HERE COMES CHARLIE MOON

HERE COMES CHARLIE MOON

written and illustrated by
Shirley Hughes

Lothrop, Lee & Shepard Books
New York

For John

Printed in Great Britain.   First U.S. Edition 1986.

1   2   3   4   5   6   7   8   9   10

Library of Congress Cataloging-in-Publication Data

Hughes, Shirley.   Here Comes Charlie Moon.

Summary: Charlie Moon spends the summer at the beach with his aunt, who owns a novelty shop, and his cousin Ariadne, who is not his favorite person.
    [1. Aunts—Fiction. 2. Cousins—Fiction. 3. Humorous stories] I. Title.   PZ7.H87395He 1986   [Fic]   85-24125

ISBN 0-688-06401-9

1

Charlie Moon's Auntie runs a joke shop at the seaside. It sells things like comic hats, masks, rubber spiders, fake flowers that squirt water at you unexpectedly, and cushions that squeak when you sit down on them. The narrow shop front faces the sea. "JOKES AND CARNIVAL NOVELTIES" it says, and underneath, "Jean Llanechan Jones", which is Charlie's Auntie's name. It's easier to say the middle bit properly if you are Welsh, as she is. You have to spit it out rather than say it.

Charlie himself lives in a big city with his Mum, who is in the hairdressing business. There are no jokes in her shop, only a row of lady customers sitting wired up to domed space-helmet drying machines, cooking slowly to lobster red as they flick through their magazines. Charlie tends to trip over their feet whilst skateboarding through the shop from the back room to the street. They don't like it. It puts them off coming. By the end of the first week of the summer holidays Mum's patience has snapped, and Charlie is off to his Auntie Jean's at Penwyn Bay. He can't take his skateboard because it weighs down the suitcase too much. It's too full already, as Charlie is a smart dresser. He wants to pack four changes

(5)

of trousers, his T-shirt with Superman on the front, and his red-and-white cap with the big peak. Also his snorkel and mask in case he wants to do some underwater swimming.

"What do you want to pack all that for?" asks Mum, forcing down the suitcase lid by sitting down on it with all her weight. "You can't see anything under water at Penwyn Bay—it's too muddy."

"I might. There might be a big fish or a seal. One of those got washed up on the beach once. I saw a picture of it in the *Penwyn Bay News.*"

"You don't need a mask and a snorkel to look at seals," Mum tells him, but they get packed all the same. "You're to help Auntie Jean with the washing-up, and in the shop if she asks you to," Mum goes on. "And don't forget to make your bed properly instead of just dragging the covers up as you do here. Ariadne's going to be there," she adds.

This is not good news for Charlie. Ariadne is his cousin. She is only two years older than he is but it seems more like five because she is so clever. Not stuck up exactly, but her Dad is a very important man who writes things in the newspapers and she reads a lot of books. Charlie likes a good book too, of course, but his mind

often seems somehow to slide off the page and he finds himself doing something else. He once read a book about a cave-man which was great. He'll read that again all right when he's got time. Ariadne being at Auntie Jean's means that she will be sleeping in the best room at the top of the house which looks out to sea, and will be sitting about reading all the time, or saying things that make people feel uncomfortable. She has two favourite words, one is "pathetic" and the other "typical". (Pretty pathetic and typical to go round with a name like Ariadne, come to that, thinks Charlie privately.)

Still, it isn't bad at Auntie Jean's.

The jokes and carnival novelties are all over the place as usual. Rows of rubbery masks are hanging up behind the counter—not the underwater kind, but funny ones of red-nosed clowns, Frankensteins, gorillas and suchlike. In the passage behind the shop are piles and piles of boxes full of crackers, indoor fireworks, magic sets and squeakers that you blow out at people to make them feel jolly. Not even Auntie Jean knows what is inside some of these boxes. In fact, she has a lot of trouble finding things. She often runs out of things to eat, too. This happens on the first afternoon of Charlie's visit.

"I'll just be popping out for a loaf and some fish fingers for tea," she sings out, climbing into her red coat. "And I might just be dropping in at Mrs Goronwy Lewis's on the way back, just for ten minutes, see. Look after the shop, won't you? Everything's priced, and all you've got to remember is to give the right change out of the till and to be ever so polite to the customers."

"I don't suppose there'll be any," says Ariadne, after Auntie's footsteps have tittupped away up the prom. "There hardly ever are. This shop's going bankrupt, if you ask me."

She stretches out on the old sofa in the back room, with a book and Einstein, the old ginger tom cat, on her stomach. From here, with her head propped up, she can see through the open door along the passage to the shop. Charlie has disappeared. All is very still. The afternoon sun lies quietly on the dusty shop floor, and outside the sea washes gently on the stones. Suddenly a strange moaning is heard. It rises to a louder moan, then to a throaty roar. A shuffling creature on all fours advances down the passage, and a monstrous face covered in green hair appears round the arm of the sofa.

Einstein merely twitches one ear.

"You are *pathetic*," says Ariadne, calmly turning over a page.

Charlie takes off the monster mask which he has borrowed from the shop, and gets up off his hands and knees. He hadn't really hoped that Ariadne would think he was a proper monster, but at least she could have pretended for a bit. It would be more fun than just lying about with a book and not talking to people. He's just about to tell her so, too, when the shop door opens with a loud clang, and in come two boys. They are sandy-haired, piggy-eyed and look as though they might be brothers. Both of them are wearing striped jerseys, hooped like barrels around their wide middles.

"Can I help you?" asks Charlie in his best shop-assistant manner, hands spread out on the counter. Ariadne, still reading, wanders out from the back room.

One of the boys starts to finger some false noses and other small items in the show-case by the shop door. The bigger one asks rudely to see some trick card games like the ones in the window. These are kept on the very top shelf behind the counter, so Charlie fetches the little step-ladder and climbs up to get the box. As soon as he has come down the boy says he has changed his mind and wants to try on a Frankenstein mask. This is even higher

up behind the counter, but after Charlie has had some
trouble reaching it the boy decides that it's much too
expensive and wants to buy some invisible ink instead.
Charlie, sighing deeply and trying hard to remember
what Auntie Jean said about being polite to the
customers, dives under the counter to find the box of
invisible inks. It's dark under there, and a lot of boxes
fall out on top of him. Some scuffling and sniggering is
going on at the other side of the counter.

"Hey, stop it! Put that back!" shouts Ariadne suddenly.

Charlie pops up his head to receive a jet of water in
one eye from a water pistol. As he's shaking the water
out of his face, he sees both the boys helping themselves
from the show-case. Ariadne is round the counter in a
flash, trying to stop them. The show-case starts to wob-
ble, false noses and moustaches fall on the floor and
confetti flies about all over the shop. As she leaps forward to steady the case the two boys are off out of the
shop door and away up the prom, stuffing stolen packets
of stink-bombs into their pockets. Ariadne rushes out
after them on to the pavement, white with rage.

"Thieves! Robbers!" she shouts, and, under her
breath, *"Typical!"*

"I'll get them!" cries Charlie. "I'm the fastest runner in the world! You stay here and mind the shop, Ariadne, while I go after them!"

And he starts off after the boys, legging it like a stag. He can see their striped back-views bobbing up and down in the distance. They're weaving in and out of the shelters, looking back over their shoulders now and again. They know by now that they are being followed. Under the railings, slithering down the sea-wall on to the beach, round the back of the beach-huts, up the steps, back on to the prom again they run. Charlie comes behind, his hair flopping about all over his scarlet face. He really is a good runner, very light and quick. The two boys are not. They are a lot bigger and heavier than Charlie, and they're already getting puffed.

As he runs Charlie starts to wonder what he'll do if he catches them up. He hadn't thought of this before. Now he remembers that there are two of them and only one of him; he's already a long way from the shop. He wishes he had somebody with him. Even Ariadne would be better than nothing. If only he could see a policeman somewhere . . . but they all seem to have gone home for tea.

Now the boys have dodged completely out of sight.

Charlie, cautious and puzzled, pants on. Suddenly, both
of them pop out from behind a shelter, grinning right in
his path. Charlie stops short. They all face one another.
Then . . . . *crack! crack! crack!* Three stink-bombs
explode on the ground. Charlie reels back, holding his
nose, as the boys disappear up a side road, whistling and
jeering. He is left standing there helplessly as the evil-
smelling cloud rises about him. At this moment two
ladies, one large and the other small, appear as though
by magic from the other end of the shelter. They both
have handkerchiefs pressed to their noses.

"Whatever's that awful . . . ?" begins one, but the
small one starts on Charlie at once.

"You ought to be ashamed! I don't know why boys
like you can't find anything better to do than to go about
ruining other people's pleasure."

"Oh, come on, Mona, it's getting worse."

"One can't even admire a lovely view in peace these
days. For two pins I'd take you along to the nearest
police station and give you in charge for vandalism."

"It's putting me off my tea."

"You've got no sense of decency any of you. Letting
off a thing like that in a public place. I don't know what
they teach you in schools these days but it certainly isn't

reasonable behaviour. At your age I wouldn't have
dared . . ." and so on and so on.

Charlie says nothing. It doesn't seem worth it. Angry
ladies never want to have things explained to them anyway. Luckily the smell is being borne away by a brisk sea
breeze. At last they hurry away up the prom, the small
lady still glaring angrily back at him over her handkerchief.

There's nothing left for Charlie to do but begin the
weary trudge home. Rather to his surprise, Ariadne is at
the shop door, anxiously looking out for him.

"You O.K., Charlie?"

Charlie tells her the story. He's too tired to make it a
good one, but he can't resist adding:

"I caught those boys up, anyway, didn't I? I told you
I could run."

"I hope they don't come back," is all Ariadne
answers.

2

The next day is bright, with white clouds blowing about the sky like washing escaping from the line. Charlie and Ariadne are sitting on the very end of the pier. Charlie likes to lean right over the rail and watch the sea smashing and crashing against the girders below, but Ariadne doesn't. She tries hard not to look through the cracks between the boards under her feet at the heaving water. The ironwork is all rusty and barnacled and smells of dead fish. It gives her the creeps. Instead she looks back at the Penwyn Bay sea front. The little houses look like toy town, all washed different colours—Auntie Jean's joke shop, the Paradise Fish Saloon, the shop that sells souvenirs and seaside rock, and, at the end of the row, Carlo's Crazy Castle.

This used to be a shop front like all the others, but now it has a false front, painted up to look just like a real castle, with pointed windows and battlements above. A big arched doorway with a portcullis opens on to the pavement. All round it are pictures of kings and queens, skeletons, gypsies, and masked headsmen with axes. Loud notices invite people inside: "SEE INTO THE FUTURE! YOUR FORTUNE TOLD FOR 25p!" "DON'T MISS

CARLO'S WORLD-FAMOUS WAXWORKS! SENSATIONAL AND EDUCATIONAL!" At the side of the entrance is a little glass pay-box, with a smaller notice saying "Closed".

At this moment the trim figure of Mr Carlo Cornetto himself appears at the pay-box window. He turns round the notice so that it reads "Open". Then he steps out in his shirt-sleeves and stands glancing up and down the prom. At one of the castle windows above his head another face appears, that of Mr Cornetto's old dog, Lordy. He sniffs the air with his large black nose, settles down on to his two front paws, and gazes solemnly out to sea. Nobody is about on the prom, only the wheeling, crying gulls. Far up at the other end of the front, beyond the shelters, in a windswept garden of its own, stands the Hydro Hotel. This has a large, grand, red-brick frontage with a great many windows, balconies and turrets, and a long glass veranda running down its entire length. Inside it one or two elderly ladies and gentlemen can be seen sitting in basket chairs, sipping cups of coffee. They, too, gaze out to sea, like castaways scanning the horizon for a friendly sail. Further still, down on the beach, the children of St Ethelred's Holiday Home are playing noisily, digging sandcastles and pouring water all over them-

selves, and one another. The student in charge is crouched in the shelter of a bit of sea-wall, trying to read a newspaper. It is an unequal battle with the wind, which keeps carrying bits of it away. Every few minutes he leaps to his feet to separate squabblers and try to wring the water out of their sopping clothes.

"Not many customers for the shop today," says Ariadne. "Typical, really."

"The coach tours can't park on this side of the bay," says Charlie. "And anyway, they've got really good things over the other side at Penwyn—dodgems and big dippers and fruit machines and all. There's a ghost train too. I wish I had the money to try them. How much money have you got, Ariadne?" he adds hopefully.

"Don't like dodgems much. And I'll bet the ghost train's pathetic," says Ariadne. She doesn't want Charlie to know that she wouldn't dare to go in the ghost train, it's far too scary.

At this moment the joke shop door opens, and Auntie Jean pops out like a cuckoo from a clock, waving them in to lunch. It's fish and chips, Charlie's favourite. This is an extravagance which happens when Auntie Jean forgets to cook anything and has to make a last-minute dash to the Paradise Fish Saloon. They eat in the

crowded back sitting-room, at a wobbly green-topped card table which has a cloth put over it at meal-times. Besides an old sofa and a great many fat armchairs, the room has an old-fashioned coal grate, a treadle sewing-machine on a stand, and a permanent smell of frying. The bold pattern of poppies on the wall-paper is mostly hidden by the various fancy costumes which hang about the room on pegs. These are left over from the time when Auntie Jean worked at the Royalty Theatre. Now it is closed, and the actors and actresses have long since gone away, leaving a good many of their costumes, hats and wigs behind.

"Those boys who stole my stink-bombs have been bothering Mr Cornetto," Auntie Jean tells them as they munch their chips. "He found them trying to get into his place the back way, but old Lordy barked at them, and they ran away. He says they're the two Morgan boys from over at Penwyn. Their Dad runs the Amusement Arcade. No-good boyos, they are. Just let them show their faces here again and I'll give them what for!"

"I don't know what they want to hang about here for," says Ariadne. "They don't need to pinch things from us, when amusement arcades make so much money."

"It's all gambling and razz-me-tazz these days," snorts Auntie Jean. "Penwyn was a very select resort when I first came here—lovely it was. Very high-class hotels, tea dances, band playing every afternoon in the Esplanade Gardens, and shows at the Royalty, of course. Lovely audiences we used to have—packed houses every night."

"Did you act on the stage, Auntie?" asks Charlie.

"Oh no, dear. I was a dresser. Helped the ladies into their clothes, hooked up their corsets, mended their tights, that sort of thing. Mr Cornetto used to go on the stage. He was an acrobat—ever so clever he was."

"I'd like to do that. Or be a conjuror, that'd be even better," says Charlie. "I'd like to put a lady in one of those boxes and pretend to saw her in half."

"Shouldn't think you'd get any lady to let you try," says Ariadne.

At this moment the shop door clangs, and Mr Cornetto himself steps in. He looks downcast. Even his neat black moustache droops at the corners, and his sad brown eyes resemble those of his old spaniel dog, Lordy.

"Cup of tea, Mr Cornetto?" asks Auntie Jean, tea-pot poised.

"Thanks, I won't say no, since you're offering, Mrs

Llanechan Jones. Just closed my place up again for a long dinner-hour, things are that quiet. Hardly worth opening up at all." Mr Cornetto is an Italian, but he sounds Welsh, like Auntie Jean, because he learnt English in Penwyn Bay. "Old Lordy's on guard, looking after things, like. Business has been bad, very bad. My Historical Waxworks, my Hall of Mirrors, people aren't wanting them as they used to. It's all roller-coasters and bingo, see. And now I'm going to have to take down my fortune-telling sign, too. Gypsy Queen Rosita has upped and left me without a word of notice. Gone into business on her own account in Llandudno."

He sups up tea through his moustache and wipes it sadly and carefully on a clean handkerchief.

"*There's* cheeky for you! I could have told you!" cried Auntie Jean. "Gypsy Queen Rosita, indeed! When we all know quite well that she's Mrs Bronwen Evans from the dry-cleaner's in Station Approach! And as for being able to tell the future—why, even old Einstein here could do better." At the sound of his name Einstein, who is lazily extended like a long ginger scarf along the back of the sofa, twitches the tip of his tail and opens one green slit of an eye. "In fact, a great deal better," adds Auntie Jean with respect. "No, don't you mind about *her*, Mr Cornetto. It's good riddance, if you ask me. And with business not being too bright here at the shop either, I'll help you out part-time, like, if I can find my crystal ball."

Auntie Jean is very good at fortune-telling. To prove it, she takes Mr Cornetto's cup and turns it gently in her hands, peering into the tea-leaves at the bottom.

"What does it mean, Auntie?" asks Charlie, leaning over her shoulder.

"Now let me see. You can't get it all at once, you know, Charlie. Looks like a little storm cloud over here, I'm afraid . . . but this is interesting. A person of some importance—a lady, I think."

"Looks more like a poodle-dog to me," says Ariadne.

"No, it's a lady. There's no mistaking her. A relative of yours, perhaps, Mr Cornetto?"

Mr Cornetto is unhelpful.

"No ladies in my family. Not living, that is."

"Perhaps it's a ghost?" suggests Charlie.

"It's a dog. I can see his ears sticking up."

But now Auntie Jean lets out a cry of discovery.

"Well I never, Mr Cornetto! Surely to goodness, I wouldn't have thought it!" she gasps.

"What is it, Auntie?"

"I see a love affair in this cup, as plain as plain. Two hearts as one!"

"Is *that* all?" says Charlie, disappointed.

"And look here! I can see a pound sign! That means money, of course. *There's* lucky for you, as plain as the nose on your face!"

She holds out the cup triumphantly. Mr Cornetto doesn't seem greatly cheered by this news.

"Well, I'll be glad if you'll help me out with the fortune-telling in the afternoons," is all he says. "Clairvoyants being difficult to come by at short notice, so the agency tells me."

They are interrupted by the sound of the shop door being quietly opened. Two figures shuffle in the doorway. It's the Morgan boys again. Slamming down the teacup, Auntie Jean looms out of the back room, hissing with fury. She can be very fierce indeed when she wants to be.

"You leave my stock alone, or I'll have the law on you, and that's only the start!" she spits. "Don't think I don't know your face, Dai Morgan, and yours too, Dylan Morgan, *and* where you live. Get out of this shop before I throw you out myself, and don't come back here or I'll . . ."

But the Morgan boys are gone before she can tell them

what else she's going to do. The others, grouped behind her in the passage, breathe sighs of relief and admiration.

"Thank goodness for that," says Charlie. He doesn't want to have to chase those Morgan boys all over again.

As it happens, the rest of the afternoon turns out quite differently for him.

"Now, I want one of you two to do a little errand for me," says Auntie Jean presently. "There's this box of crackers and paper hats that needs delivering at the Hydro Hotel. The manageress is planning a Carnival entertainment—trying to cheer the place up, see. Though how she's going to manage it with that lot that's staying up there, I don't know."

"I've got to write a postcard home," says Ariadne quickly, eyeing her book.

As there seems to be nobody else to offer, it's decided that Charlie shall go. The box he has to deliver is a large one, not very heavy, but bulky enough. Charlie sets off up the narrow streets behind the prom, carrying it first under one arm, then under the other, and ends by balancing it on his head with his cap turned back to front. Like this he climbs up the imposing front drive of the Hydro Hotel, marches up the front steps, and enters the

large hall, blinking in the dimness. It is completely
empty. There is a big counter of polished wood with a
vase of flowers on it, and a notice saying "Reception.
Please ring." Charlie dumps down his box, adjusts his
cap, and rings. Nobody comes. He rings again, loudly.
Still nobody. While he waits, Charlie begins to wander
about, admiring the little pink lamps on the round tables
and trying out the huge padded armchairs. Far away in
the hotel he can hear voices and the faint noise of vacu-
uming. He comes to a wide staircase, sweeping down
into the hall and dividing into two flights at the bottom.
This might be so that two people could race each other
and see who reaches the hall first, thinks Charlie. In the
middle is a huge, old-fashioned lift shaft, like a great iron
cage with a glass box inside it. The lift doors stand open.

Charlie steps inside and presses the button marked
"Basement". Immediately the doors close, the lift gives
way pleasurably under him, purrs downwards, and stops.
At once Charlie presses another button marked "4th
Floor". The lift glides upwards. He has been in plenty of
lifts before, of course, but in this one you can see the
staircase moving past through the glass. He presses
another button—fifth floor this time—then down again
to the ground floor.

"Five, four, three, two, one—we have lift-off," mutters Charlie, and up he goes again to the fourth floor, changes his mind, presses the third floor button in mid-flight. Then he starts to go up and down like a yo-yo, pressing all the buttons at random, and watching the bannisters slide giddily by. He is at the very top of the building, and dropping down to the basement again for the sixth time, when the lift suddenly gives a jolt, a shudder, and stops abruptly between floors. Charlie presses all the buttons, one at a time. Nothing happens. He tries again. Still the lift doesn't move. He struggles to open the doors, but they remain firmly shut.

"I'm stuck," says Charlie to himself.

And then, aloud, with panic rising, "Oh, help, I'm stuck!"

3

Downstairs in the hotel lounge Mrs Cadwallader and her sister-in-law, Miss Mona Cadwallader, are taking afternoon tea. They sit surrounded by a dense jungle of palms, looking out at the windy sea. Inside the temperature is tropical. The guests at the Hydro have to be kept very warm, like tomatoes under glass. Miss Mona perches upright on the edge of her chair. She resembles a neat bird of prey, now and again dipping daintily into her teacup. Mrs Cadwallader, a large lady with blonde curls arranged like an enormous pile of bubbles on top of her head, lies back among the cushions. A great many necklaces and rings sparkle gaily about her, but her mouth droops.

"Boring," she says. "A really boring view I call this—all those waves. Makes me seasick. They're not even blue! And it's not as though there's many people on the beach either. If we were in the Bahamas, now, that'd be a different matter."

"It's time for our walk, Connie, dear," murmurs Miss Mona, carefully ignoring these remarks, all of which she has heard before. "Which shall it be? A stroll on the pier, or up to the headland?"

"I'm sick to death of the headland," answers Mrs Cadwallader crossly. "We go there every afternoon when we don't go on the pier, and either way we get blown to bits. I'm sick of the prom, too. Nothing happening there, either, except nasty little boys dropping stink-bombs all over the place. It isn't as if there were any good slot-machines. Why don't we go over to Penwyn this afternoon and give the Fun Fair a try? Might see a bit of life over there at least. We could find out what's on at the cinema."

Miss Mona raises her eyebrows. She has two pairs. The real ones are plucked and the others are thinly pencilled in half an inch higher up.

"I can't think why you're always wanting to go over to that vulgar place, Connie. It's completely tasteless and without any kind of attraction, as far as I can see. We did come here for a quiet holiday for old times' sake, after all."

"Quiet all right! More like a graveyard. Penwyn isn't a bit like I remember it years ago. Anyway, I keep telling you I don't need a rest. I'm just bored stiff."

Miss Mona smiles patiently and consults her tiny watch.

"If you don't want to join me in a walk, dear, I think

I'll just pop out for a little blow on my own. I'll see you upstairs half an hour before dinner. Don't forget to allow plenty of time to change, will you? You know the manageress likes us to be punctual."

"Punctual, indeed!" snorts Mrs Cadwallader. "Nothing worth being punctual *for*!"

She remains in her chair, staring gloomily out of the window. Presently she sees Miss Mona in a headscarf, setting briskly out along the prom. Mrs Cadwallader rises and looks about the lounge for someone else to talk to, but there is nobody left except old Colonel Quickly, snoozing underneath his newspaper. Sighing, she wanders into the hall and rings for the lift.

As she waits for it to arrive, she is already wishing that she hadn't spoken so crossly to her sister-in-law. Mona's patience is often a reproach to her. They have lived together in hotels ever since Mrs Cadwallader's husband died, and have had many such conversations. Mrs Cadwallader is very rich, because her husband left her all his money, and the family jewellery. Miss Mona, on the other hand, is not well off at all. So she accompanies Mrs Cadwallader from one hotel to another trying to get her to behave properly, in a genteel manner. She has very little success. Mrs Cadwallader doesn't care what people

think of her, and misses her old knock-about life terribly. She was on the stage before she married her husband, Caddy, who was a devil-may-care fellow, who liked driving about in a fast open car and played tennis in sparkling white trousers. How unlike his sister, Mona, he was. And how Mona had disapproved of the way they both whirled about the world, going to parties, cinemas and motor-racing, and doing nothing but enjoy themselves.

Mrs Cadwallader sighs again, thinking of those happy, long-lost days.

"Boring, that's what it is," she says, and rings for the lift again. Nothing happens. She is very put out. Her room is on the fourth floor, and she hates walking upstairs. What is more, this is the third time the lift has failed to arrive since she has been staying at this hotel. She looks about for somebody to complain to, but there is nobody. Frowning, she sets off up the stairs. She has reached the half-landing between the second and third floors when she hears a knocking noise. She stops and looks up the stairwell. She can see the bottom half of the lift with a pair of legs inside it. It is from here that the noise comes. Walking up a few more stairs, she peers in through the thick plate glass. Charlie Moon's face looks back at her like a goldfish from a bowl.

"I'm stuck," he says. But Mrs Cadwallader can only see his lips move silently, making him look even more like a goldfish than before.

"What are you doing in there?" she asks severely.

"I'M STUCK!" shouts Charlie. He is red in the face with anger and fright. He bangs on the lift door, points up, points down, rattles the door as hard as he can.

"Aaaaah, I *see*! You're *stuck*," says Mrs Cadwallader more kindly. She doesn't recognize Charlie as the boy on the prom, under the big peak of his cap. "Well, you're not the first one. That lift is a danger to the public. A disgrace, that's what it is."

She signals to him to stay where he is, and goes off to get help. Charlie hasn't really any other alternative, so he settles down to wait as patiently as he can. After a while, back comes Mrs Cadwallader with the hotel handyman. He in turn goes off to fetch a ladder, grumbling in Welsh, and disappears up into the roof to wrestle with the ancient machinery that works the lift. Mrs Cadwallader remains, now joined by one or two other guests, smiling encouragingly at Charlie and making cheery remarks. She has quite forgotten her bad mood in all the excitement. To Charlie the time seems endless. He wonders if he will ever get out of this horrible glass

box, but he feels too exposed to give way to despair. Instead he pulls the peak of his red-and-white cap down over his eyes and huddles in a corner, ignoring everyone.

At last the lift gives a violent jerk. Then it moves shakily down to the second floor landing, and the doors open. Charlie is free at last! By this time a small crowd has gathered, including the manageress herself, who is extremely cross. Everyone wants to know what Charlie has been up to, getting himself stuck in the lift like that and causing so much trouble. Eyeing the stairs and longing to get away, he starts wearily to explain about the box of Carnival novelties, which he hopes is still sitting in the hall. But at this moment Mrs Cadwallader steps forward and, much to his embarrassment, throws an arm protectively round his shoulders.

"Don't keep asking him questions. Can't you see he's all upset, poor little chap? Quite green round the gills, he is. You'll be lucky if his Mum doesn't prosecute. I know I would if I was her, an' all!" And with this, she steps smartly back into the lift, pulling Charlie with her, presses the button marked "Basement" and they both disappear instantly from view.

The basement floor of the Hydro Hotel is almost entirely

occupied by the ballroom. These days it remains nearly always empty, save for a lot of dust and rows and rows of tiny gold chairs, ranged about the walls like ladies waiting for a dance. At one end of it, in a place where an orchestra used to sit, is a glossy black piano. Charlie and Mrs Cadwallader step out into an echoing half-light, with a faint lingering smell of face-powder, stale tobacco smoke and linoleum. Then Mrs Cadwallader finds a switch and the room is filled at once with a piercing rose-coloured glow.

Charlie is very relieved to have been rescued from the lift, and from trying to explain what he was doing in there in the first place, but he is not at all pleased to find himself alone in a ballroom with Mrs Cadwallader. He is hot, confused and exhausted, and he wants to go home. What's more he is troubled by the uncomfortable feeling that at any moment he may be recognized. So far it's clear that he hasn't been, but under these lights it's a bit risky. This could mean more trouble.

"Thank you very much. I think I'd better be getting back now," says Charlie. "My Auntie's expecting me."

But Mrs Cadwallader pays no attention to this. She lights a cigarette in a long green holder.

"Terrible hotel, this," she tells him, "what with that

lift breaking down, and the hot-water pipes juddering and gurgling in my bedroom at some ungodly hour in the morning, and the food stone-cold half the time. I'd walk out tomorrow if I thought I could get in anywhere else."

"It's just that my Auntie . . ."

"When things aren't going wrong or breaking down, it's like a graveyard. All those old fogies. I like a bit of life myself. Music, dancing, that sort of thing." She puffs out cigarette smoke in the direction of the piano. "I was in the theatre, you see."

"Yes, so was my Auntie. But . . ."

"Very slim I was in those days. You live round here, dear?"

"I'm staying at my Auntie's. As a matter of fact she's expecting . . ."

"On holiday, are you?"

Charlie nods.

"So are we, me and my sister-in-law. I like the big resorts, but she likes it very quiet, very refined. When we were in Spain last year Mona was the one who complained. Too noisy and too hot, she said, and the food gave her a liver attack. Talk about a moaner! She never stopped! Didn't like the guests in the hotel—said they weren't the right type—didn't like the dancing." She

glances at the empty ballroom. "I love a dance myself. I wonder when they last had one here?"

Before Charlie can answer Mrs Cadwallader sets off across the huge shiny floor, humming a tune, and holding her cigarette holder out at arm's length with her other arm about the shoulders of an imaginary partner. Her high-heeled shoes swerve in all directions making a complicated pattern of steps.

"I think I ought to be . . ." calls out Charlie after her, but she doesn't seem to hear. She reaches the piano. Sitting down, she balances her cigarette-holder on the end of the key-board, removes her rings, and strikes up a thrilling chord. Then she bursts into song.

"WALTZ-ing WALTZ-ing, HIGH in the clouds.
ON-ly YOU and I in the clouds . . ."
carols Mrs Cadwallader sweetly.

Charlie sits down on one of the little gold chairs, defeated. She sings on and on, playing more runs and trills on the piano than anyone could have believed possible. Between verses she beams over at him, for all the world as though he were a proper audience. Charlie begins to feel desperate. At last delivery comes. The lift doors at the other end of the room open, and out steps Miss Mona. Mrs Cadwallader's song falters

in mid-flow, and her hands drop from the key-board.

"So here you are, Connie," says Miss Mona quietly. "I hope you realize what time it is? Dinner is in ten minutes." She looks coldly at Charlie. "Is this the boy who got stuck in the lift? I heard all about it from the manageress herself, when I came in from my walk. She was really annoyed. We've been looking all over the hotel for both of you. What on earth have you been doing in here, anyway?"

"Just having a bit of fun," says Mrs Cadwallader defiantly, but she shuts up the piano lid all the same. "I was just giving this little lad a song or two."

Miss Mona fixes Charlie with a beady eye.

"I feel I've seen you before," she says. "What is your name?"

"Charlie Moon," answers Charlie, pulling down his cap even further over his eyes.

"Where do you live?"

"I'm staying with my Auntie who runs the Joke and Carnival Novelty shop along opposite the pier, and I think if you don't mind she'll be expecting . . ."

"*I* know who you are!" snaps Miss Mona, looking at him more closely under the peak. "You're the little vandal who was behaving so disgustingly on the prom

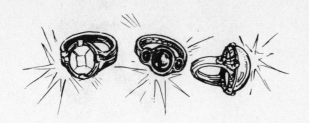

yesterday. You're an obvious trouble-maker, that's clear. I suppose you thought you could come trespassing in this hotel and making more mischief without being recognized? Now, listen to me. You're to leave here at once and if I hear of your causing any more trouble I'm going straight to the police."

"Oh, come on, Mona," says Mrs Cadwallader. "He wasn't doing anything."

"*Straight* to the police, do you understand? Now come along, Connie, we must change. We're terribly late already."

Taking Mrs Cadwallader's arm, Miss Mona sweeps her into the lift. As the doors close, Mrs Cadwallader catches Charlie's eye over the top of her sister-in-law's head, and gives him a big wink.

Left alone at last, Charlie breathes a great sigh of relief. It has been a long, difficult afternoon. He is sick to death of the Hydro Hotel and everyone in it. He never wants to see any of them again. But, as he turns to go, something catches his eye, twinkling on top of the grand piano. Drawing nearer, he sees three rings lying there—very expensive-looking rings with stones nearly as big as boiled sweets. Mrs Cadwallader has left them behind!

"You still here, then?" says the hotel handyman sternly.
Charlie has collided with him as he tears upstairs with
the three rings in his pocket. "You'd better not let the
manageress catch you. She's in a black, bad temper,
indeed. And, look you, don't go messing about with that
lift again, or I'll have you for sure. I've got enough to do
here without young tomfool boyos like yourself tinker-
ing about all over the place."

"Those two ladies," pants Charlie, "they've just gone
upstairs. I've got to catch them!"

"If it's the Cadwallader ladies you mean, they've gone
to their rooms, no doubt, as it's nearly time for dinner.
What do you want them for, anyway?"

"There's something I've got to give them. It's important."

"Well, right-ho then. But you're to come straight
down again, mind. They're on the fourth floor. I can't
recall the big lady's room number off the top of me head,
but the other one's in Number 404."

"Thanks!" shouts Charlie over his shoulder. He's
already sprinting up the next flight of stairs, two at a
time. No more lift journeys for him.

The Hydro seems to have as many rooms, passages
and stairs in it as an enchanted palace in a fairy tale, and

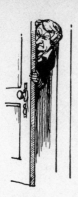

to be just as confusing. Reaching the fourth floor, Charlie takes off from the main staircase, scurrying like the White Rabbit down long corridors, and counting the room numbers backwards under his breath as he passes. Nobody is about. Most of the guests are already gathered for dinner downstairs. Through open doors he glimpses marble bathrooms, dignified mahogany beds with starched white sheets, and the occasional small, startled reflection of himself in a huge wardrobe mirror. At last he arrives at room Number 404 and knocks timidly.

Miss Mona's questing, bird-like face appears almost immediately.

"Is this intended to be some sort of joke?" she says angrily, before Charlie can get in a word. "You have no business to be up here, as you well know. I won't tell you again. Kindly leave these premises *at once*, or I'll call the manageress."

"I . . . the other lady . . ."

"You mean my sister-in-law? She's dressing for dinner. What do you want with her?"

"I found . . . I mean, she left these behind on the piano!"

Charlie plunges his hand into his pocket and pulls out

the three rings. They lie winking and sparkling on his palm. Miss Mona looks at them silently for a moment.

"I see," she says, in a slightly altered tone. "That was most careless. I will see that they are returned at once."

She takes the rings into her own hand and half closes the door. Then she adds, through the crack:

"Thank you for returning them promptly. Now please LEAVE HERE AT ONCE!"

The door is then closed firmly in Charlie's face, and he is left standing alone in the corridor. Tired as he is, he breaks into a wild, capering dance, throwing his cap about, thumbing his nose, and pulling hideous faces at the closed door. Then, turning away, he starts to try and find his way back to the main staircase. At last he can go home for his tea.

4

"Lovely bit of material, that is," says Auntie Jean, holding up a gentleman's tailcoat, one of the many items of costume that she keeps in her back sitting-room. "Bit of moth under the arm here, but good as new otherwise."

She blows the dust off the shoulders of the coat, and it rises in a great cloud.

"What's that purple dress, Auntie, with the black lace on it?" asks Ariadne. She and Charlie are sitting side by side on the sofa, eating sticky buns.

"Oooooh, that's a dream, that is. It's an old-fashioned costume, once worn by the leading lady in a musical play at the Royalty. A real picture she was in it, too."

"It's just like the sort of dress the ladies in my book are wearing. I'd love to sweep about with that train thing behind."

"What's that shaggy brown one over there?" Charlie wants to know.

"Some sort of animal suit, I think, Charlie. It was for the pantomime one year, if I remember right. Looks as though it needs a bit of a patch in it when I get a moment. Lovely on, though."

Auntie Jean is in good spirits. She loves going through

the old costumes and reminding herself of happy times in
the theatre. It is the day after Charlie's adventure in the
lift, and it has been a successful one in the shop. A party
of trippers strayed in during a shower and all bought
false noses to cheer themselves up on the way home.

"I've got some lovely pork chops for tea," she tells
them. "And chocolate ice-cream to follow—a treat, see.
Why don't you slip along and ask Mr Cornetto if he
wants to come round and join us? He looks as though he
could do with a good meal. I don't believe he cooks
anything proper, there on his own."

Charlie and Ariadne stroll up the prom, still chewing
the remains of their buns. The sun has come out, warm-
ing the damp pavement under their feet, and catching
the sails of two little boats, dipping along optimistically
in the bay. The tide has gone out, leaving behind it a
glittering expanse of rich, salty mud, garlanded with
dark seaweed. In the middle distance, the children from
St Ethelred's Holiday Home are straggling along the
water-line, with melted ice-lollies dribbling down to
their elbows. They stop now again to poke about
amongst the driftwood, or push one another into the
pools. The student in charge, his trousers rolled up to the
knee, moves up and down his flock like a sheep-dog,

herding them home to bed. Their voices echo across the bay as in an enormous bathroom.

Charlie and Ariadne arrive at Carlo's Crazy Castle to find Lordy in charge of the pay-box, his fore-paws on the till. He greets them with loud barks, which bring Mr Cornetto hurrying to the entrance. He winds up the portcullis to let them in.

"Well, there's kind of you, I'm sure!" he exclaims, when they deliver Auntie Jean's invitation. "I'm just closing up here. I'd a few people round earlier, but it's pretty quiet on the whole. Want to see round for free, while you're here, do you?"

He leads the way into an entrance hall, strangely decorated in a style half way between a medieval castle and a tea-bar. There are suits of armour, a life-sized bear carved out of wood, some plastic-topped tables and chairs, and rows of old-fashioned slot-machines ranged about the walls. There is also a gilt mirror or two, some shields and helmets, and a piano with pictures of storks and flowers painted upon it. At one end of the room is an archway, covered with a heavy velvet curtain, marked "HALL OF WAXWORKS". Another archway at the other end has a curtain of beads with a notice saying "GYPSY QUEEN ROSITA. FORTUNE-TELLER AND CLAIRVOYANT".

(41)

But over this is pasted another notice with the words "Temporarily Closed".

Mr Cornetto ushers them proudly into the Hall of Waxworks. Two rows of shabby lurching figures are arranged along low platforms, behind looped silk cords. Ariadne, who is fond of History, knows who most of them are without having to read the labels—Napoleon, Queen Elizabeth the First, Sir Francis Drake, Nelson, Christopher Columbus. There are other, more sinister characters, too—Dick Turpin, the highwayman, with a cocked hat and levelled pistols, and, at the far end of the room, a tableau of Mary Queen of Scots with a masked Executioner, who looks as though he is getting ready to chop off her head.

"That one's great," says Charlie. "He's really scary!"

"I like her dress—all those pearls," agrees Ariadne.

The waxworks return their gaze with glassy eyes.

"And now, the Hall of Mirrors," says Mr Cornetto, throwing open another door. They pass through it into a maze of their own reflections. In one mirror Charlie is as round and fat as Humpty Dumpty. In the next he is as tall and thin as if he had been pulled out like chewing-gum, and his eyes seem to meet in the middle of his head.

Standing together, a little further on, he and Ariadne appear as two giants, their feet miles away, their bodies ballooning out round the middle, and their giggling faces flattened out like saucers.

"Bet you look like that when you're grown up," says Charlie. "You could get a job on the telly as one of those monsters from outer space."

But Ariadne doesn't bother to answer back. She has already moved on to see, reflected over and over again, an endless vista of herself, in which every small movement turns her into a forest of arms or an army of legs.

"Like being a centipede," she murmurs. "But where do I—or rather, where does *it*—end?"

But Mr Cornetto is already leading the way through the mirror maze into another smaller room with more slot-machines in it and a huge weighing-machine which says "I SPEAK YOUR WEIGHT", past a small door marked "Private", which leads upstairs to the little flat where he and Lordy have their living arrangements, then back to the entrance hall.

"Now, I've just got to lock up and give Lordy his supper," says Mr Cornetto, when they have admired everything. "I won't be long. You two go ahead and tell your Auntie I'll be along about a quarter to seven, if that

suits. Lordy can stay here and look after things while I'm out."

The evening sunlight on the airy prom seems very reassuring after the dusty fantasies of Carlo's Crazy Castle.

"Those slot-machines are a bit pathetic," says Ariadne on the way back, "sort of old-fashioned. I've seen *much* better ones in the Amusement Arcade over at Penwyn. They have lots of flashing lights and things, and you can win a whole pile of money on them—well, sometimes you can. I liked the Hall of Mirrors, though."

"And the waxworks," Charlie adds, "specially that one with Queen Elizabeth having her head chopped off."

"Mary Queen of Scots, Charlie. Don't you know *any* History?"

"Course I do. But we haven't done that bit. At our school it's all projects—Roman walls and roads and that. Not many battles. We did some good stuff once about the Barbarian Hordes sweeping across Europe, but then we had a new teacher and went back to roads again. Do you think Mr Cornetto gets many customers?"

"Doesn't seem like it. As bad as Auntie Jean's—absolutely typically pathetic, in fact," says Ariadne, greatly

cheered, as always, by being able to use both her favourite words at once.

The shop door is already closed, with the blind pulled down, so they go round the back, to be met by the delicious smell of frying pork chops and onions. Auntie Jean is in her little kitchen, darting about in a cloud of smoke and steam, with Einstein weaving excitedly round her legs. Hungry as hunters, Charlie and Ariadne start to lay the table in the sitting-room, putting on a clean checked table-cloth. There is a loud, insistent knocking at the shop door.

"That'll be Mr Cornetto, I expect," calls out Auntie Jean. "He's early. Just let him in, will you, Charlie, dear?"

But the shadow Charlie sees on the blind at the end of the passage is far too big to be Mr Cornetto's. When he unlocks the door and opens it there, as large as life, is Mrs Cadwallader, beaming and looking very grand in pink and pearls. She sweeps right past him into the shop.

"I'm *so* glad I got your address right, dear," she says. "I felt I just had to thank you personally for returning both my rings to me yesterday. It really was silly of me to leave them lying about like that. Mona was furious, of

course. I'm always doing it, you see. The things I've lost! You wouldn't believe it! Valuable, too. The trouble is, I can never remember what I've put on in the morning when I take it off at night. And then, of course, when I find I've lost something, it's too late to look for it. Little Scatterbrain, my poor late husband used to call me. But you saved me this time, and no mistake. I wanted to give you this, as a little token of my appreciation."

She presses a pound into Charlie's hand, and airily waves away his thanks.

"So this is your Auntie's shop," she continues, looking about her at the masks and false noses. "I like a joke myself—always have done. Poor Mona's got no sense of humour, I'm afraid, and that's a fact. Only the other day . . . Good heavens above!" Her flow of chatter stops abruptly, as though she has seen a ghost. Over the top of Charlie's head she has caught sight of Auntie Jean, standing in the doorway in her big flowered apron.

"I don't believe it!" gasps Mrs Cadwallader, clutching her pearls.

"It can't be . . . !" cries Auntie Jean.

"Well, I never did!"

"Connie!"

"Jean Jones!"

"Indeed to goodness me, where on earth did you spring from after all these years?"

Charlie, open-mouthed, just manages to step neatly out of the way as the two ladies come together in the middle of the shop in a hearty embrace.

"Come right inside, Connie, dear," says Auntie Jean, ushering Mrs Cadwallader through into the back room and sitting her down in the best armchair. "You children, lay another place at the table. We've another guest for tea!"

As the two ladies fall to chattering and laughing and exclaiming both at once, like a pair of noisy parakeets, Charlie and Ariadne, goggling with astonishment, try to piece together the explanation for this surprising reunion. Bit by bit, they find out that Mrs Cadwallader, in her days on the stage, once played a summer season at the Royalty Theatre. Auntie Jean was working there then as a dresser, and the two became firm friends. But after Mrs Cadwallader married her rich husband they somehow drifted apart, and haven't laid eyes on one another again until this very moment.

"Well, fancy your being the lady that saved this young scamp nephew of mine from being stuck in the lift yesterday," says Auntie Jean. "What a small world it is,

indeed! And you one of those posh folk staying up at the Hydro!"

"I'm staying there with my sister-in-law, Mona. But they're an unfriendly lot up there. Nobody talks to anybody. Things aren't a bit like they used to be. Even the old Royalty's closed, I see."

"Yes, sad isn't it? The dear old Royalty. The times we had there, Connie! All that rush and excitement before the curtain went up, and you such a picture in those white tights and all those sparkling sequins!"

"Oh, it's such years ago now. But seeing you here makes it seem like yesterday," says Mrs Cadwallader happily. "Do you remember, Jean, that roll of drums from the orchestra pit, then *smash* went the cymbals, and up I went into the air, as light as a feather!"

"And I was always that frightened in case you fell off! There you were on that pyramid of strong men, all standing on top of one another's shoulders, with you at the very top! I never knew how you had the nerve, Connie, really I don't!"

"Oh, that was nothing to me in those days. I was a dancer, as you know, before I joined that troupe of acrobats. And I could sing too, of course. In fact, I was

(48)

running through a few old numbers with your nephew here. Quite carried away I was. But I'm a bit out of practice for acrobatics, I'm afraid—put on a little bit of weight recently."

"You remember Mr Cornetto of course?"

"Carlo Cornetto? Why, of course. He was one of the troupe, you know. Lovely acrobat, he was, but couldn't speak a word of English, as I remember. Just used to smile and show his white teeth."

"He's retired now and settled down right here in Penwyn Bay. Took a fancy to the place, learnt to speak English lovely, and now he's running the Crazy Castle down at the far end of the prom. I'm expecting him here at any moment, as a matter of fact. Oh my goodness, those pork chops will be burned if I don't have a look at them. Is that him now? Quick, children, run and let him in!"

Mr Cornetto has changed into his best suit and is wearing a silk bow tie that resembles a large yellow spotted butterfly. He is so surprised to see Mrs Cadwallader that for the moment he forgets all his English and bursts into a flow of excited Italian, clasping both her hands and kissing them over and over again. At last Auntie Jean manages to sit everyone down at the table. Mr Cornetto soon regains his command of English, and

throughout the meal all three grown-ups talk and talk, reminding one another of past dramas and excitements behind the scenes at the Royalty, of old friends long since forgotten, and telling one another over and over again how little they have changed, and how they would have known each other anywhere. Charlie and Ariadne attack their food in silence, and escape as soon as possible into the kitchen to finish up the remains of the chocolate ice-cream in peace.

"I'm getting a bit sick of the old Royalty," says Ariadne, licking her spoon thoroughly. "They don't half go on about it—that Mrs Cadwallader especially. Can't she talk!"

"Wait till she starts singing," answers Charlie.

"I don't see how anybody could have lifted her up into the air, not even a whole troupe of acrobats. You'd need a *crane*, if you ask me."

"She's given me a quid, though."

"Oooooh, lucky! What for?"

"Getting her rings back for her. It's funny, though . . ."

"What's funny?"

"When she thanked me just now, she said for both her rings."

"Well?"

"But there were three of them, all whoppers. I remember them quite well because I had them in my pocket."

"I expect she made a mistake."

"She's only got two of them on now. I looked when Mr Cornetto was carrying on, using all those foreign words and kissing her hands."

"Perhaps she's left the other one somewhere else by now. She seems pretty dotty, if you ask me."

At this moment they both become aware of a lull in the flow of chatter coming from the sitting-room. They stop licking their spoons and look towards the door. Einstein, who has been finishing up the remains of the pork chops under the sink, also looks up, his ears cocked. Then the lull gives way to another much more piercing sound. Einstein, with bristling fur, bolts like lightning through the pantry window. Mrs Cadwallader has started to sing.

5

It's Thursday afternoon—early closing day at the Joke and Carnival Novelty Shop—and all is confusion in the little back room. Auntie Jean, wearing a gypsy costume and shawl, with a bright scarf tied over her hair and a great many jangling bracelets and beads, is pulling everything about in a frantic search for her crystal ball. She is expected at the Crazy Castle to tell fortunes at two o'clock sharp. In the passage the piled-up boxes are spilling out their contents all over the floor—packets of paper streamers, gigantic false teeth and plates of plastic fried eggs are everywhere, but no crystal ball. Charlie, who started by trying to help, has found a camera which shoots out a rubber snake when you press the button, and he is trying it out on Einstein, who sits solidly on the dresser, his eyes half closed in disgust. In the midst of it all, Ariadne is curled up in an armchair, reading.

"Come out of that book, Ariadne, do, and give us a hand," cries Auntie Jean in anguish. "If I can't find the dratted thing I won't get any fortunes told today!"

Ariadne drags her eyes unwillingly from the page. Balancing herself with one hand on her book, to keep

her place, she hangs upside down over the seat and peers under the sagging frill.

"There's something under here, I think. Oooooh, what a lot of fluff!" She gropes about and pulls out a long pink silk scarf and a green cigarette case, along with a cloud of dust.

"Now whatever have you got there?" says Auntie Jean, bending down to inspect them closely.

"Not your crystal ball, I'm afraid. Perhaps they belong to Mrs Cadwallader. I think this scarf matches the dress she was wearing when she came the other evening."

"I believe you're right! That's her cigarette case for sure."

"She must be awfully absent-minded, leaving her things behind all the time, I mean. First the rings that Charlie found, and now these. Typical, I suppose."

"You'd better slip up to the Hydro and give them back to her. Pop them into a package with her name on it, so you only have to leave them at the reception desk."

"Oh, all right," says Ariadne, "I'll do it when I've finished this chapter."

Auntie Jean resumes her search, with a great deal more commotion and fuss. At last the crystal ball is discovered under a bit of blanket in Einstein's cat

basket. It has to be well washed and polished before being restored to its black velvet coverings. Ten minutes late already, Auntie Jean whisks her shawl straight and bustles away up the prom.

"Walk up to the Hydro with us, Charlie," asks Ariadne, throwing down her book and yawning.

"No thanks, not likely," says Charlie. "I'm not going up there again. I hate the place. And anyway the Old Moaner might catch me."

"How pathetic," says Ariadne. "Oh well, I suppose I'll have to go on my own."

Having put Mrs Cadwallader's things into a package and addressed it carefully in large curly letters with her felt pen, Ariadne strolls off with it under her arm, up the hill to the Hydro. Today the reception desk in the big hall is attended by the manageress herself, who is busy with a typewriter and a great deal of paper work. She hardly raises her eyes as Ariadne enters.

"I suppose you've come about the job," she says. "It's only the one time, you know. We need extra help because of the Carnival Lunch we're having, but otherwise we're perfectly well suited. How old are you?"

"Thirteen," says Ariadne promptly. She is really only twelve, but can never resist adding on a year.

The manageress looks her up and down over her glasses.

"Well, I really had someone older in mind. I'm not allowed to employ anyone of your age on a permanent basis, of course. You look like a reliable girl, though. It's just to help the waitress and clear up afterwards. Can you lay tables?"

"Yes, I can."

"Well, you might do. I'll take your name and address at any rate."

"I'm Mrs Jean Jones' niece, from the joke shop on the prom, but I haven't come after the job," Ariadne manages to tell her. "I've brought this. One of the ladies staying in this hotel, Mrs Cadwallader, left some things behind when she came to see us the other evening." And she puts the package down on the desk.

"Oh, I see. Why didn't you say so before? Mrs Cadwallader and her sister-in-law are in the Palm Lounge at this moment, I believe, so you can give them to her now if you like. It's just over there, to the left."

Ariadne shuffles her feet and stays where she is.

"Well?" asks the manageress. She has already turned her eyes back to her papers.

"I'd like to take the job if you want someone. I could

help the waitress like you said. And I can wash up, too."

The manageress looks at her again. After a bit she says:

"Well, as I know your aunt I'll give you a try. But only if she gives her permission first, mind. We'll pay you 75p an hour and you get a free meal. I'll need you here on Saturday week at twelve noon, sharp. Don't forget now."

"I'll be here," says Ariadne. Inwardly she is surprised at herself for making such a sudden decision. As she writes her name and address, she is already wondering what Auntie Jean will say, and if she will allow her to work at the Hydro. She hadn't really meant to ask for the job, or to pretend to be older than she is. Somehow the words just slipped out. But the manageress has already returned to her work, and the matter seems to be settled. Picking up the package, Ariadne goes off in the direction of the Palm Lounge.

At first she can't see Mrs Cadwallader anywhere. The huge room is nearly empty. Walking all round it, she soon hears low, angry voices coming from a little alcove, hidden by a forest of foliage.

". . . vulgar in the extreme," hisses one voice, and Mrs Cadwallader answers:

"You're always trying to spoil my fun, Mona. Just because I meet up with a couple of old friends and have a chat about old times, you have to try and stop me."

"I just don't think they're suitable people for you to mix with," says Miss Mona. "That awful joke shop. I've never seen so much cheap rubbish in all my life. And who is this Italian with his ridiculous side-show?"

"It's not ridiculous. He'd be doing very good business if he were over at Penwyn. Just needs a bit of brightening up, that's all. He was a lovely acrobat, too, in the old days, when I first knew him. He could do four back somersaults and land on his hands, no trouble at all, and then jump up into the air like a jack-rabbit! You should have seen him!"

"I'm very glad I didn't. I should have thought you'd want to forget about your previous career, now you have a social position to keep up."

"It was *me* that Caddy married, after all," retorts Mrs Cadwallader, "and *he* didn't give tuppence for social position!"

Before Miss Mona can answer this, Ariadne clears her throat loudly and edges round the potted palms, with the package held out before her.

"Well, I never did!" says Mrs Cadwallader, after greeting her warmly. "What's this? Don't tell me I left

these behind at your Auntie's? I've been looking for them everywhere."

Miss Mona eyes Ariadne with annoyance.

"Really, Connie," is all she says. "Isn't that the cigarette case you had as a wedding present? I wish you'd try to look after your things better. Give those to me right away. I'll take them upstairs for you."

Mrs Cadwallader ignores her.

"You're a good lass," she tells Ariadne. "A pair of good kids, you and your cousin. I'm grateful to you both. Here's a pound. And as you're here, I'll walk back with you to your Auntie's for a breath of air."

"She's telling fortunes at Mr Cornetto's this afternoon," Ariadne tells her. "She's ever so good at it. But I don't need a reward, really."

"Take it, dear. Never refuse money when it's honestly earned. So Jean's fortune-telling at the Crazy Castle, is she? I think I'll go along there, then, and see how she's getting on." She rises to her feet, and winds the long pink scarf several times round her neck with a flourish. "Cheerio, Mona. See you later, alligator, as we say in Show Business!"

Miss Mona does not answer, but the tilt of her small beak of a nose makes her feelings very plain.

6

"More life! More sparkle! Music, lights, razzle-dazzle!" exclaims Mrs Cadwallader, waving her scarf about.

"What was that last one again?" asks Mr Cornetto cautiously.

"Razzle-dazzle. Excitement, glitter—*you* know. It's what this place needs."

"Oh, yes. I see." Mr Cornetto chews his moustache thoughtfully.

The Crazy Castle has closed for the day, and they are all eating ham sandwiches at one of the little round tables in the entrance hall. Auntie Jean is still wearing her gypsy costume. There have been more visitors than usual that afternoon, and she has seen a good many exciting futures in her crystal ball.

"Apart from a lick of paint and a good smarten up, you need some kind of special attraction," continues Mrs Cadwallader. "Something that'll bring in the crowds—as well as Jean's fortune-telling, of course."

"What about lots of gambling-machines?" says Ariadne. "Or a space-machine like they've got over at Penwyn?"

Mr Cornetto shakes his head.

"Things like that cost a lot of money, and I've hardly any in the bank. The bank manager keeps writing me letters about it."

"When Mum and I went to the circus," says Charlie, "there were people outside the big tent, dressed up, beating a drum and shouting 'Roll up! Roll up!' to get people to come inside."

"My word, that's given me an idea, Charlie!" cries Mrs Cadwallader excitedly. "You know those old costumes you've got at your place, Jean? We could have an Old Time Night here—you know, dressed in old-fashioned costumes, and getting people to join in with songs that they all remember. I could lead the singing—and you can still play the piano, can't you, Carlo?"

"Oh yes, indeed. But I'm not sure . . ."

"We could open up the portcullis here and have coloured lights. And we could smarten up the waxworks, too, while we're at it. Re-hang the curtains, polish up the mirrors, all that kind of thing. I'll help with the expenses."

"And I'll help with the sewing if I can," says Auntie Jean. "Come on, now, Mr Cornetto. Things are that slack at the joke shop this season, I'll have to close down if we can't attract some more people over here some-

how. Anything's worth a try. Would you children be kind enough to help out, d'you think?"

"I could paint up some of the pictures of kings and queens and things on the front of the building," offers Ariadne. "I'm good at painting. I hardly ever go over the lines."

"I'll polish up the magic mirrors, if you like," says Charlie.

"You're all very kind," says Mr Cornetto, "very enthusiastic. All right, we'll give it a try, then."

"*There's* sensible!" cries Auntie Jean, giving him a clap on the shoulder, which makes him swallow his sandwich the wrong way.

"I'll come down first thing tomorrow morning," Mrs Cadwallader tells him, "and we'll get started. I must practise all my old songs. Oh, I'm so excited! It'll be just like old times, Carlo, dear."

The grown-ups embark upon a long chat about plans. Charlie and Ariadne wander off with Lordy to look at the sea. The tide is coming in fast. Lordy, forgetting his age and dignity, gallops about in the fading light like a skittish judge, barking wildly at sea-gulls. They follow him along the tide-line, sometimes pausing to throw a stone or two out to sea.

"She's a bit *overpowering*, Mrs Cadwallader, isn't she?" says Ariadne. "She and that other lady—her sister-in-law, or whoever she is— were having a real old row up at the Hydro this afternoon. In fact, they're both rather bossy, if you ask me!"

"Mr Cornetto doesn't seem to mind being bossed," says Charlie.

"Pretty pathetic of him. You know what, Charlie . . ."

"What?"

"I told a bit of a fib this afternoon to the manageress at the Hydro."

"What fib?"

"Well, I pretended I was older than I was so that they'd give me a sort of waitress job. It's only for one day, to help with the Carnival Lunch. I hope Auntie Jean'll let me."

"Don't see why not. But I can't think why you want to go and work at that old place. I bet they're as mean as anything. They'll probably make you wash up piles and piles of dishes and then not pay you anything."

"Oh, dear. I hope not. I thought it seemed sort of exciting, like the girl in my book who is all alone in the world and has to go and be a governess in a big house."

"Well, don't get in the lift. You might get stuck in

there for ever and not be found until there's nothing left but your whitened bones.''

"Don't worry. I won't go near it," says Ariadne with a shudder.

The following morning the portcullis of Carlo's Crazy Castle is lowered, with a notice on it saying "Temporarily closed for renovations. Watch out for our Grand Reopening and Old Time Night on Thursday next!" Inside Mr Cornetto, in rolled-up shirt-sleeves, is already at work rearranging the entrance hall, nailing up strings of coloured lights and bringing in more chairs from the outhouse at the back. Charlie is the first to arrive.

"Ariadne's looking after the shop today while Auntie Jean gets on with the sewing. She's found some smashing costumes and she's altering 'em now," Charlie tells him. "She's got ever so many of them—animal suits and uniforms too, with medals and that. Where's the ladder and bucket?"

Mr Cornetto has put them out ready for him in the Hall of Mirrors, so he gets busy at once. The mirrors are very dirty and fly-blown, and difficult to clean, too, because they are not flat like ordinary ones. He finds that when he has too much soapy water in his cloth, it

slops down the surface and dries in streaks. But he soon discovers that if he wrings the cloth out and lets the clean glass dry until just the right moment, he can get a good polish on it. He rubs away, moving his head up and down now and again to observe his reflection melt from a squashed-lemon shape to dripping candle-wax. From the entrance hall comes the sound of Mrs Cadwallader's voice. She has come to practise her Old Time songs on Mr Cornetto's piano. Charlie finds that the water in his bucket is already dirty. Rattling the handle noisily and whistling, he climbs down the ladder and goes out through the Hall of Waxworks to refill it at the outside tap in the back yard.

As he opens the back door there is a sudden rush of footsteps, and a dustbin goes bowling over with a clatter. He is just in time to glimpse a figure—or is it more than one?—disappearing over the wall. Before Charlie can open the gate and peer out into the back alley-way, whoever it was has disappeared round the corner. Charlie doesn't feel like giving chase. He sets the bin upright again and picks up most of the escaped rubbish. Thoughtfully he slooshes the bucket of dirty water down the drain, refills it and goes back inside, locking the door carefully behind him.

Auntie Jean has just arrived, Mrs Cadwallader has stopped singing, and together they are in the Hall of Waxworks, surrounded by costumes, hats and wigs. Auntie Jean is crawling on her hands and knees round Mrs Cadwallader, trying to pin her into a long dress with a train. Mrs Cadwallader's coat and her long string of pearls are draped over the waxwork figure of Christopher Columbus, who is also wearing a brown bowler hat tilted at a rakish angle.

"There was somebody in the yard just now when I went outside," Charlie tells them, but neither pays much attention. Auntie Jean's mouth is too full of pins for her to answer properly. Out of the side of it she says:

"Mmemmer mime, mear, I mmespeck issa sray hat."

"But it wasn't a cat," Charlie insists.

Auntie Jean removes a few pins.

"If it's those Morgan boys up to their tricks again . . . ! Oh well, they've gone now, I hope. Make us a cup of tea, Charlie, there's a good boy."

"But I'm trying to wash the magic mirrors."

"Can you pull it in a bit more at the waist, Jean?" says Mrs Cadwallader. "My word, this is great! I feel just like something out of 'Upstairs Downstairs'."

Auntie Jean's mouth is full of pins again.

"Breave imm bleeply, mmear," she tells her.

Charlie sighs, plumps down his bucket, and goes off upstairs to the little kitchen where Mr Cornetto does his cooking. There he finds Lordy lurking under the table. Uneasy about all the preparations which are afoot, he has retired from his usual job commanding the pay-box.

"A rotten watch-dog you are, too," Charlie tells him sternly, slamming the kettle down on the stove. "We could have twenty burglars in here before *you'd* notice anything, sulking under there."

Lordy's baggy eyes droop tragically. Charlie relents and gives him the remains of Mr Cornetto's breakfast to cheer him up. As he makes the tea, he decides that he must tell Mr Cornetto himself about the intruders. But when he arrives downstairs with the tea-tray, he hears angry voices upraised in the entrance hall. Peeping round the plush curtain, he sees all three grown-ups huddled together like cornered sheep, confronting the bristling figure of Miss Mona. Her small form is compacted with fury, and she is poking her neck forward like a goose about to peck somebody.

"You're making a perfect exhibition of yourself,

Connie! You must be mad even to *consider* appearing in public dressed like that. Poor dear Caddy would turn in his grave if he could see you—thank heavens he was spared it."

"Rubbish, Mona," retorts Mrs Cadwallader bravely. "I was dressed up when Caddy first met me, except that then it was silver tights. He'd be *glad* to see me enjoying myself, so there!"

"You're far too old for it now—you look quite ridiculous!" Miss Mona tells her cuttingly.

Mrs Cadwallader looks momentarily dashed, but Mr Cornetto puts in gallantly:

"Not at all, she's elegance itself! She's helping to give my place a new look for the Grand Reopening. Excitement, glitter, razz-me-tazz—*you* know . . ."

There is an icy pause. Miss Mona turns her gaze upon him, and he shrinks beneath it.

"I most certainly do *not* know," she says at last. "Neither do I *wish* to know. As far as I am concerned my sister-in-law is making a silly spectacle of herself dressed up like that. I thoroughly disapprove of her being associated with a . . . a . . ." She looks about as though another stink-bomb were wafting under her nose ". . . *venture* of this kind. It's embarrassing. Take that dress off,

Connie, and come along back to the hotel."

"No, I won't."

"I insist, Connie."

"But I'm having such a good time . . ."

"I'm not leaving here without you."

"You'd better go, Connie," says Auntie Jean, giving her a nudge. "I've fitted the dress anyway. Let's have it back, and I'll go on with the alterations."

"Oh, all right," says Mrs Cadwallader crossly. "But I'm coming back and . . ." She glares at her sister-in-law . . . "nobody's going to stop me!"

A strained silence follows in which Mrs Cadwallader goes off to change. Behind his curtain Charlie wonders why grown-ups have to get so worked up about such unimportant things. He decides that it's not the right moment for tea, so he takes the tray back upstairs and drinks some himself. By the time he comes down again Mrs Cadwallader and Miss Mona have already gone.

"I saw it in the tea-leaves the other day—a dark cloud, a little spot of trouble," remarks Auntie Jean, as she packs up the costumes in the Hall of Waxworks. "Never mind, Mr Cornetto, we mustn't let that Miss Mona interfere with our preparations. Nasty, stuck-up old thing! *I* thought Connie looked lovely myself, a real picture."

"A picture indeed," agrees Mr Cornetto. "She hasn't changed at all since the old Royalty days—not one little bit. But I'm worried about our Reopening. We couldn't get on without her."

"Of course we won't have to get on without her. As far as Connie is concerned, the show always goes on! Now stop bothering yourself, Mr Cornetto, and try this bowler on for size."

Auntie Jean lifts the brown bowler hat off the head of Christopher Columbus and hands it to Mr Cornetto, who puts it doubtfully on to his own. It is not a good fit. Being much too small, it perches on his head uneasily. He hands it over to Charlie, who, trying it on in turn, finds that it comes well down over his ears and nearly covers his eyes, so that he can hardly see out. All the same, he decides he'll wear it as a change from his peaked cap.

"Good gracious me! Well I never!" exclaims Auntie Jean. She's not looking at Charlie, but at the figure of Christopher Columbus, round whose neck she has noticed Mrs Cadwallader's pearls. Carefully Auntie Jean removes them and holds them up to the light.

"*There's* careless! They're real ones, too! That Connie doesn't seem to care tuppence about all this valuable

jewellery her husband left her. Only the other day she left her expensive cigarette case behind, and there were those rings that Charlie found. It's just like her. Once I even caught her using a diamond brooch instead of a safety-pin because she couldn't be bothered to sew on a button!"

"My Mum goes mad when I lose things," says Charlie, "even though she's just as bad herself. You should see her looking for her glasses, or her purse when the milkman calls for his money."

"But *real* jewellery!" says Auntie Jean, and she clicks her tongue in a shocked way. "Well, I shall just have to take these pearls back to my place and put them away safely until I see her again. But I wouldn't be surprised if she doesn't even notice she's lost them!"

"She's a remarkable lady," says Mr Cornetto, "a truly remarkable lady."

Barmy, more like it, thinks Charlie to himself, but aloud he says nothing. Tipping the bowler on to the back of his head so that he can see better, he picks up his bucket and goes back to the magic mirrors. What with one thing and another, he has quite forgotten about the intruders in the yard.

7

The next few days are hard work for everybody, cleaning, sewing, polishing, painting and hanging curtains. The Crazy Castle gradually takes on a new look, and so do the waxworks in their smart costumes, refurbished by Auntie Jean. Ariadne spends hours on a ladder painting up the figures on the outside of the building. She gives the kings beautiful new crowns and moustaches, the queens golden hair and jewels in all colours of the rainbow, and the skeletons grinning green teeth and eyes which glare horribly from their black eye-sockets. Groups of curious passers-by on the prom stop now and then to watch.

"I'd like to do a prehistoric monster—a Diplodocus or a Tyrannosaurus Rex—but there isn't room," she tells Charlie, who is standing at the bottom of the ladder to hand up paint-pots and give advice.

"Even if there was, people would think there were monsters inside and it wouldn't be fair," says Charlie firmly. "Mr Cornetto's ordered two new pin-tables, though," he tells her. "They're arriving today. It's beginning to look great in there."

It certainly is. Strings of coloured lights lend romance

to the entrance hall, where newly-painted chairs and tables are grouped about invitingly. Even Mr Cornetto seems excited. He has put up posters about the town announcing the Reopening, and he is going to accompany Mrs Cadwallader on the old piano, wearing a loudly checked suit and waistcoat and a large flower in his buttonhole. Mrs Cadwallader herself has somehow managed to escape Miss Mona's eye to practise with him whenever possible. But each time somebody has to be on guard in case her small but alarming figure is seen stalking up the prom. So far, all is well. Everybody is in good spirits except poor Lordy, who seems to be more and more upset by all the changes to his old home.

"We'd better take him round to Auntie Jean's, Mr Cornetto," says Charlie on the day of the Reopening. "He can stay the night in the kitchen. Einstein always goes out then. I'll give him a bowl of dog-meat."

That evening the portcullis of the Crazy Castle is drawn up and the lights shine out. Charlie, dressed in a red soldier's jacket covered in medals, has taken Lordy's place in charge of the pay-box. A small crowd starts to collect. They drift inside to play with the slot-machines and gaze at the waxworks and magic mirrors. Then out steps Mr Cornetto, and sits down at the piano. He strikes

up a few loud tinny chords, and launches immediately into the sort of tune that makes you want to keep time with your feet. Now Mrs Cadwallader appears, beaming and splendid in her long old-fashioned dress, and starts to sing. Her voice carries out over the darkening prom. A much larger crowd gathers. There is a certain amount of giggling curiosity. But gradually one or two people start to join in the choruses. Mrs Cadwallader carries them along, coaxing and encouraging. She has clearly never enjoyed herself so much for years.

"There was I,
Waiting at the church,
Waiting at the church,
He's left me in the lurch . . ."

Business is brisk in the tea-bar. Ariadne flies about in a starched cap and apron, serving snacks. A queue forms for the fortune-telling booth.

"It's a giggle, anyway," says a girl to her friend. "Better than hanging about."

"I had my fortune told. It's much cheaper than over at Penwyn, and she told me I was going to marry a rich rock and roll singer and live in America."

"Those old slot-machines are a real laugh. There's one with a kind of peep-show with old-fashioned bathing beauties."

"She's going to sing again. Keep us a seat over there, will you, Sandra?"

A small party of ladies and gentlemen from the Hydro Hotel pass by and drop in to see what's going on.

"Isn't that one of the guests from our hotel? My dear, I didn't know she was an entertainer."

"I *thought* I recognized her. What's that she's singing? I think I remember it . . ."

"Quite takes one back, doesn't it? Just like the seaside when I was a gel."

"Get us some cheese and onion crisps, Brian."

"Ask her if she knows 'Yellow Submarine'."

"Makes a change from television anyway . . ."

"A week's takings in one evening!" cries Auntie Jean triumphantly at breakfast the following Sunday morning. "Mr Cornetto and I counted it up late last night. It's getting better all the time. Wait till I tell Connie, she *will* be pleased."

"If the Old Moaner finds out she won't like it, will she?" says Charlie. He hasn't forgotten the angry words

he heard between the two ladies when he was hiding behind the curtain.

"No, I'm afraid she won't, Charlie. She'll try to put a stop to it if she can."

"Typical!" snorts Ariadne. "Just when Mr Cornetto is on the verge of gold beyond the dreams of avarice."

"What's that mean?" Charlie asks through a mouthful of cornflakes.

"Rich, of course. I read it somewhere."

"P'raps we'll all be rich. Mrs Cadwallader's really good at making people join in with the singing, isn't she? You'd think they'd be sort of shy, but she won't let them be."

"I wish I could play the piano like Mr Cornetto," says Ariadne. "Bouncing your hands up and down over the keys like that looks so easy, but it isn't really. I've tried."

At this moment Lordy, who has been sitting under the table, bounds out to greet his master, as Mr Cornetto himself bursts in through the back door. He looks very unlike his usual self, with hair on end and shirt tails hanging out at the back.

"Why, Mr Cornetto, whatever is it, indeed?" asks Auntie Jean anxiously.

"Burglars! Wreckers! My place . . . it's been broken into in the night!" Mr Cornetto tells them wildly.

Leaving their breakfast at once, they all hurry round to the Crazy Castle. Lordy rushes inside ahead of them pretending to be a bloodhound, nosing the ground and growling deep down in his throat. The entrance hall is a mess. Tables and chairs have been turned over, a curtain has been half pulled down and is hanging lopsided, paper cups and plates are scattered everywhere, as though someone has been playing a pointless game with them, and nearly all the remaining food has been trodden underfoot on the floor. One of the slot-machines has been damaged and the carved wooden bear is lying on his side in a pool of lemonade.

"The waxworks!" screams Auntie Jean at once, rushing over to the archway. "Oh, thank heavens they're safe!"

"I locked that door last night before I went to bed, so whoever it was never went in there," Mr Cornetto tells her. "They must have climbed in through the little window by the back door. They've been in the Hall of Mirrors, though."

They have indeed. Sticky handprints, splodges of butter and melted ice-cream cling to all the carefully

(76)

polished surfaces. On one big central mirror, written in what looks like tomato sauce, are the words "Thank U Verry Much!"

Looking at it, and remembering all his hard work, Charlie suddenly feels very weary. Then he remembers too about the time when he was polishing those very mirrors and heard somebody in the back yard. Now, too late, he tells them all about it.

"If it's those Morgan boys . . ." says Auntie Jean, but even she is too depressed to get into one of her rages.

"Typical!" mutters Ariadne.

"There's no proof that it's them," says Mr Cornetto. "It could have been anybody."

"I'm sorry I forgot to tell you that day, Mr Cornetto. There seemed to be such a lot going on at the time."

"It can't be helped, boy. Don't you think any more about it. One thing, though. None of the money's gone. I put that where no one'd find it in a hurry. In fact, the more I think of it, nothing of any value's been stolen. They don't seem to have been those sort of burglars."

"Vandals!" exclaims Auntie Jean. "You'll have to report it at the police station, Mr Cornetto."

"Yes, indeed, I suppose I will."

They all follow him back to the entrance hall, where

he stands among the wreckage looking smaller than usual. All the happy triumph of the morning has drained away. Nobody knows where to begin. Only Lordy rushes about, busily growling and sniffing. Ariadne opens the piano and picks out a few plaintive notes.

"Whoever it was never got round to spoiling the piano, anyway," she says. "I *am* glad."

"Well, thank heavens it's Sunday and we're closed until tomorrow," says Auntie Jean briskly. "Gives us a bit of time to help you get cleared up, Mr Cornetto. I'll have to put off Chapel till this evening, but I've no doubt the Lord will make allowances. You put on the kettle and make us a cup of tea, Ariadne dear, and we'll get started."

Mrs Cadwallader joins them just as cleaning-up operations are getting under way. She is in great spirits, and is not at all put out by the scene that greets her.

"I've seen worse," she says. "We had terrible trouble with burglars once when I was on tour. Took all the costumes and all, I hadn't a rag left to wear." She hangs up her smart coat and starts to roll up her sleeves.

"I've given Mona the slip this morning," she tells them gleefully. "She booked us on a coach trip to see an old country mansion, but I pretended I wasn't feeling up to it. She won't be back until late tonight. I'm afraid she's

very suspicious, though. There are rumours at the hotel about what I'm up to here, and she pretends not to hear. I'll be in trouble before long, I'm afraid, but who cares? Give us that scrubbing-brush, Jean. I'll get on with the floor while you re-hang that curtain.''

A great Sunday afternoon quiet settles on Penwyn Bay. Cleaning up the Crazy Castle has turned out be an easier job than it seemed at the beginning, and Mrs Cadwallader has rounded off the morning's work by sending Charlie out for a dinner of fish and chips for everybody, double portions all round.

Both children have now been let off for a swim, and are sitting on the beach on their damp towels, Ariadne deep in her book as usual. Charlie is trying to knock a tin can over by throwing small stones at it.

"Having burglars isn't nearly as exciting as I thought it'd be," he says. "Just a lot of mess and hard work. They didn't leave any proper clues we could follow up, like real detectives."

"They wrote 'thank you very much'," says Ariadne, without looking up.

"That's no good. I meant footprints, blood, bits of hair, proper clues like that."

"Well, there were plenty of sticky smears."

"We should have taken fingerprints," says Charlie, throwing another stone and missing.

Keeping her place carefully with a bit of seaweed, Ariadne picks up a small pebble, and, aiming it at Charlie's tin, hits it first time.

"They weren't real burglars, anyway, because they didn't take anything," she says. "And if it's those Morgan boys, which it probably is, you won't want to catch them because they're much bigger than you. It would be completely pathetic."

"I could get the police to send them to prison."

"No, you couldn't. Policemen don't send children to prison."

Charlie is thoroughly irritated.

"Well, I'll do something to them. Give them a terrible fright."

"Don't be *pathetic*, Charlie. What sort of fright?"

"I don't know. I'm thinking," is all Charlie can answer. Ariadne returns to her book.

Later, she says:

"I heard Mrs Cadwallader and Mr Cornetto arranging to go for a walk on the pier this evening. He's going to leave Lordy behind as a watch-dog."

"That's silly," says Charlie crossly. "Lordy's not much good at that kind of thing if you ask me. What do they want to go on the pier for in the evening anyway? They're neither of them interested in fishing."

"Perhaps they're going out together—you know."

"Don't be stupid. They're *old*. Anyway she's always talking and telling people what to do, and all. Nobody could want to go out with her."

"She's got lots of money and jewels and things, even if she is always losing them. Perhaps Mr Cornetto doesn't mind her going on at him. Perhaps it'll be good for him."

"Well, somebody ought to warn him," says Charlie bitterly.

"Perhaps we could make out he's got a wife already, that nobody knows about, like the man in my book. He's got one that's mad, and he keeps her locked up in the attic."

"Go on. How could Mr Cornetto have a mad wife at the Crazy Castle? There isn't room for one. He's packed out with stuff already."

"I suppose you're right," admits Ariadne reluctantly. "Well, they're going out tonight anyway, so if *you* want to give the burglars a fright, Charlie Moon, this could be your big chance."

"What d'you mean?"

"Well they're bound to come back. I read somewhere that criminals always return to the scene of their crime. So you could jump out on them wearing a mask and say 'Boo!', or whatever pathetic thing you're thinking of."

There is a short silence while Charlie considers this.

"All right, I will then."

"What, jump out at them?"

"No, something better. Give them a fright so they won't *ever* come back."

"You wouldn't dare."

"Yes, I would."

"Wouldn't. What could you do, anyway?"

"I'm not telling yet. But you'll have to help me."

"Typical! Why should I?"

"Cause I can't manage it on my own."

"What if they don't come?"

"*You* said they would," says Charlie, turning on her. "You keep talking about all those things you've read about so you can show off. So now we'll see!"

"*All right*, then. We will. Now will you get on with your pathetic plan, whatever it is, and let me get on with this story?"

8

All the houses on Penwyn Bay front, from Auntie Jean's shop on the corner up to the Crazy Castle, have back yards giving on to a connecting alley-way, which is full of old cartons, broken milk-bottles and other dubious rubbish. It's a cat's kingdom, where Einstein haunts the dustbins at night, competing noisily with his enemies for tit-bits. But this evening, at dusk, all is quiet. Not a cat to be seen. The television sets are glowing blue-white against tightly drawn curtains, and only bursts of recorded studio laughter break the silence.

Auntie Jean, after evening Chapel, emerges from the front door of her shop and hurries away up the prom in the direction of the all-night launderette in Market Street, pushing the huge pramful of dirty washing which has been lying in wait for her all week. Soon after she has departed, Ariadne puts her head round the back gate which leads into the alley. Then she creeps out, leading the shuffling hairy figure of a gorilla. It is wearing a long mackintosh and floral headscarf. Almost immediately it trips on a squashed orange, falls down on its face, and has to be helped up and dusted off.

"I tell you, I can't see properly," says Charlie's voice

crossly from somewhere inside the gorilla's mouth. "You're supposed to be leading me, aren't you?"

"All right. You'll get used to it soon. Hang on to me and try not to make such a row."

"It's too hot in here."

"Well!" says Ariadne, pulling him along. "That's typical! It was your great idea to dress up in that suit, left over from some pathetic panto at the old Royalty, and now you're grumbling about it already. I had enough trouble getting you into it."

"It's this scarf on top of the mask. It's suffocating me."

"You have to cover yourself up somehow until we get there, Charlie. Suppose we meet someone?"

"I didn't think this body part was going to be so uncomfortable. It must have been made for a dwarf."

"Hunch over a bit. It'll make you look more realistic."

It had seemed like a good idea to Charlie that afternoon to dress up in a gorilla suit, but now he's inside it he's not so sure. He's had his eye on it ever since he arrived at Auntie Jean's and noticed it hanging behind the sitting-room door. The head part he found on a high shelf at the back of the shop. It has huge grinning teeth, flaring red nostrils, and deep eye-sockets under a shaggy fringe of hair. The body part is made of artificial fur,

zips up the back, and is very dusty. Charlie thought
he had managed to get rid of most of the dust by shaking
the whole thing out of his bedroom window, but now he
realizes he hasn't been very successful. He seems to be
hovering all the time on the edge of a sneeze. What's
more, it smells nasty inside, and the eye-holes are too
wide apart, so he can only see out by squinting down one
nostril.

Of course Ariadne was all ready to be scathing when
he explained his idea to her, how he meant to dress up
and lie in wait at Mr Cornetto's place while he was out, in
case whoever-it-was came back again.

"What do you want a *disguise* for?" she couldn't resist
asking. "It'd be easy enough without the mask."

But she'd helped him into it and zipped him up the
back all the same. She's even admitted that the effect
was pretty good. They'd had to hide in the top bedroom
until they'd seen Mrs Cadwallader and Mr Cornetto
setting out, arm in arm in the summer dusk, for their
walk on the pier. After that, it was an all too easy job to
lure Lordy from his post as watch-dog with the help of a
bowl of dog-meat. Ariadne has "borrowed" the spare
key to Mr Cornetto's back door from its usual place on
Auntie Jean's dresser. Lordy is, at this moment, very full

and already dozing heavily in one of Auntie Jean's arm-chairs.

They creep along the alley-way and manage to reach the back door of the Crazy Castle without meeting a soul. Once again Ariadne puts the key into the lock, but she finds she has no need to turn it. She had forgotten to re-lock the door when she let Lordy out.

"Hey, wait a minute while I get these clothes off," says Charlie, struggling out of the headscarf and mackintosh. Together they fold and hide them behind Mr Cornetto's dustbin, then they creep inside the house.

At first it's too dark to see anything. They grope their way through the rear door of the Waxworks Hall. The rows of figures stand in uncanny stillness, muffled in their elaborate costumes. A faint light filters through a little cracked glass dome overhead, catching a sharp beak of a black profile here and there, a towering wig, a glittering glass eye. Ariadne finds her throat is dry, clears it, and is appalled by the loud noise it makes. It is much too quiet in here. Her superior attitude to the whole plan drains away suddenly. It seems impossible to speak in the presence of these listening shapes, and even more impossible to walk up the room between them. She flattens herself against the wall.

"Come on," says Charlie hoarsely, dragging her arm and shuffling forward. "You hide up here, behind the curtain over the archway. I'm going to be in the entrance hall."

"It isn't worth it, Charlie. Nobody's here. Nobody's going to come . . . are they?" Her voice trails off into a squeak of fright.

But Charlie is resolute. He pads off into the darkness. Unable to bear being left behind, Ariadne hurries after him, not daring to look on either side of her. She reaches the curtain and peers round it into the entrance hall beyond. She can make out only tables and chairs, neatly arranged after their labours that morning, ready for tomorrow. Charlie seems to have disappeared into thin air.

"Charlie?" she croaks into the blackness.

There is a muffled answer from the far corner. Charlie's gorilla shape is standing against the wall between the big wooden bear and a suit of armour, looking as much as possible like another waxwork figure.

"Hide behind the curtain," he hisses across the room. "We've got to lie in wait."

"But Charlie . . ."

"What?"

"Let's go home after all. I mean, nobody's going to turn up. It's all totally pathetically useless our being here."

Charlie doesn't answer.

"Mr Cornetto might come back and find us here, and we won't know how to explain."

A pause. Then:

"All right. Go, then. You go off home if you like. I'm staying."

"Don't be silly. I won't leave you on your own."

"Well, *hide*."

Ariadne retreats behind her curtain and hides. Charlie stands stiffly in his corner, as much to attention as his gorilla suit allows. Darkness. Silence. Minutes heavily passing. Voices and footsteps are heard faintly from time to time on the prom outside, but they walk on by, and fade away. In what seems like an endless tunnel of time, nothing at all happens. Every now and then Charlie can be heard snuffling inside his gorilla mask. But he is grimly determined not to give in—not for an hour at least. It was his idea, after all.

After a very long time, Ariadne is suddenly aware of a faint thud. It comes not from outside on the prom but somewhere inside the building. She listens, straining.

Then there is another noise, a slight scuffling. Then a
door opens slowly. It's the door behind her, right over
the other side of the Waxworks Hall—the one she and
Charlie came through themselves. Somebody is coming
in the same way.

Ariadne presses her hand over her mouth to stop
herself from calling out. Has Charlie heard too? Moving
the curtain very slightly, and putting her eye to the
narrow gap, she can see him still standing in his corner,
absolutely still. Behind her she can see nothing at all,
only hear the footsteps, creaking up the hall towards her.
Now a black shape blots out her line of vision, then
another. Two figures pass by, only inches away from her.
She sees a shoulder, a bit of anorak, a glimpse of an ear,
someone about her own height. They pass through into
the entrance hall. There is the sound of stumbling, of
knocking into furniture. Then voices, suddenly loud.

The Morgan boys, of course!

"Watch where you're stepping, boy. Want to get us
nicked?"

"I can't see. Where's the counter?"

"Over here, where it was before, see? Come on."

"It's breaking and entering, Dai."

"Not if they leave the door open it isn't. That's asking

us in. They ought to know better after the last time, only they're that daft."

"Where's the dog, then?"

"They haven't no dog."

"I've seen one hanging about here."

"Aaaach, come on. Let's get some grub. I fancy some crisps, anyway."

More clumsy stumbling against tables and chairs as they make their way across the hall in the dark. Then a sharp intake of breath. Slowly Charlie's arms have started to move.

"Whassat?"

"What?"

"Over there, in the corner. Something moved!"

Silence. Then:

"Getaway, it's only one of them stuffed waxwork things. We'll soon have that over."

"Not that one—the other! Hey, Dai, let's get out of here . . . DAI! It's *walking*! Aaaaaaaah!"

Slowly Charlie moves forward, all hunched up and hairy, with his arms up and his great mask-jaw poking forward out of its fringe of hair—which is the only way, in fact, he can see where he's going. He's a terrifying sight in the shadowy dark.

The two Morgan boys scramble and blunder against each other in their panic to get away from him. One knocks over a chair, nearly falls, staggers to his feet again, straight into the arms of the wooden bear which lurches forward on top of him. Letting out a yelping scream, he dodges away, so that it rocks and falls. Meanwhile Dai has bolted through the archway that leads to the other small lobby. His brother flees head-long after him. Charlie, arms clawing the air, follows relentlessly.

The Morgan boys now have no idea where they are. They crash about against the wall, knocking into slot-machines, trying to find the other door. Some glass is smashed. Suddenly a blood-curdling disembodied voice speaks right into their ears, repeating the same phrase over and over again:

"Only one person at a time, please . . . Only one person at a time, please . . ." Charlie stops short, momentarily off his guard. But then he recognizes the voice of the "Speak-Your-Weight" machine. Jolted into action, it can't stop.

"Only one person at a time, please . . . Only one person at a time, please . . ."

The Morgan boys are now nearly demented with fear.

one person at a time, please, only one person at a time, ple

Managing at last to wrench open the door that leads into the Hall of Mirrors, they hurl themselves through. Instantly they are confronted by an army of reflections, a forest of themselves, an endless moving mass of arms and legs.

". . . one person at a time, please . . . Only one person at a time, please . . ." mocks the hollow voice behind them. But as they run through the maze of mirrors, more and more grotesque versions of their own faces gibber and leer at them. Suddenly they are brought up short against what seems like a dead end, a huge mirror cutting off their escape. Now, over the shoulders of their reflections, they see the monster that pursues them, with sunken eyes, hairy arms upraised, and awful fixed grin. There's a passage leading on to the left, but here more mirrors surround them, and now there seems to be not one monster but many, great gorilla shapes leaping up, with others crowding behind, all reaching out to grab them.

"Only one person at a time, please . . . Only one person at a time, please . . ." insists the voice in the darkness.

At last another door, and beyond it they see deliverance. The back door leading out into the yard. They see

the evening sky, the ordinariness of the brick wall. With a great burst of speed, the Morgan boys are out of the door and over the wall in an instant, with Charlie still lumbering after them.

Ariadne, left behind her curtain, listens transfixed to the voice of the "Speak-Your-Weight" machine, going on and on until at last it starts to slow down.

". . . person . . . at . . . time . . . please . . . only . . ."

Then, abruptly, it stops altogether.

Ariadne puts her head out and peers through the darkness of the entrance hall at the confusion left behind by the rout of the Morgan boys.

"Charlie?" she calls quietly.

No reply.

She takes a few steps out from her hiding-place and calls again. Still no answer. Charlie has gone. She hesitates fearfully, trying to remember where the light-switch is. She starts to feel her way along the wall, searching desperately. No switch. She finds herself blundering back through the curtains of the archway into the Hall of Waxworks again. Here, at least, there is a little light. But now she is alone with those stiffly posed figures, they appear even more terrifying—Dick Turpin with his pistols raised, the Executioner with his evil axe.

To get to the back door she must somehow walk the length of the room, exposed to all those glassy eyes. She measures the distance, trying to pluck up courage. She knows that, besides the set-piece of Mary Queen of Scots, there are eight waxworks on each side of the aisle. Head down, eyes on the ground, she starts off. If you look at the feet, not the faces, it isn't so frightening. What's frightening about eight pairs of feet? She counts out of the corner of her eye. One, two, three, four, five . . . nearly there . . . six, seven . . . quick! quick! . . . eight, nine . . .

Suddenly she stops dead, her hand actually on the door handle.

Nine?

That's one pair extra.

Slowly, slowly she turns, eyes still down, and counts again. Six, seven, eight . . . She raises her eyes. Far down at the end of the hall, the end she's just come from, there is a faint rustle. The ninth waxwork is moving.

Ariadne shapes her mouth to a wild scream of fright, but no sound comes out. Flinging open the door, she bolts into the gathering dusk.

9

The lights are on over at Penwyn. The Fun Fair throws
up a harsh multicoloured glow into the sky, and snatches
of pop music can be heard across the lapping water. Mrs
Cadwallader and Mr Cornetto, strolling home along the
prom in the dark, are taken unawares by Ariadne's
sudden hurtling approach. She seems to come on them
from nowhere, blundering into them, hardly realizing
who they are. Gulping and stuttering with fright, she tells
them the whole story.

"That's all right, dear . . . you're safe now . . . never
you mind then . . .'' murmurs Mrs Cadwallader, patting
her comfortingly, though she finds all this muddled gib-
berish about gorillas, burglars and moving waxworks
difficult to follow. "What *have* these children been up
to?'' her glance says to Mr Cornetto over the top of
Ariadne's head. They both hurry back with her to the
Crazy Castle at once.

Ariadne hangs back, clinging to Mrs Cadwallader, as
they reach the front entrance. This being still locked, Mr
Cornetto produces his key, opens up the portcullis, and
strides in ahead of them. He goes from room to room,
switching on all the lights. The signs of the Morgan boys'

headlong flight are there all right, but in the Hall of Waxworks all is in order. Nothing has moved. Eight figures stare down at them from each side of the aisle and Mary Queen of Scots bows her neck to the Executioner, just as though nothing had happened.

"There *was* a ninth—I counted," insists Ariadne. "I know it was there. And it did move, I'm sure of it."

But somehow, with all the lights on, it all seems less likely. Even as she speaks, she's beginning to doubt it.

"Well, it was a daft idea of Charlie's in the first place," says Mr Cornetto, locking up the back door. "You should never have taken Lordy away from here. He's a good watch-dog—the best in North Wales, and that's a fact."

"Well, Charlie scared them off, didn't he?—those horrible Morgan boys, I mean," mutters Ariadne. "It was only when I was left all alone in the dark . . ." Her voice wobbles dangerously.

"It's been a long day, love," says Mrs Cadwallader firmly. "We're all tired out. Now come along, we'll walk you back to your Auntie's and you can get off into bed right away."

There's nobody at home when they get back to the shop.

"I wonder where Charlie's got to?" says Ariadne. "We *must* go and look for him."

But somehow her knees suddenly seem to bend under her, and she finds herself slumped in an armchair, hugging the welcoming Lordy for moral support.

"You're staying right where you are," Mrs Cadwallader tells her. "You've had enough for this evening, I should think."

Charlie is hiding in a doorway at the other end of the prom. He had known from the start that he wasn't going to be able to catch up with the Morgan boys. That wasn't the idea, anyway. Dressed in a gorilla suit, it was all he could do to manage a loping stride, which couldn't possibly match the speed they were putting on to get away from him. They've probably never run so fast in their lives, thinks Charlie with satisfaction. They'll be half way to Penwyn by now, and they won't be back in a hurry.

Charlie is so hot inside his mask, with all the running and excitement, that he feels as though he's going to melt. He struggles with it, but somehow it's anchored to the rest of the suit at the back of his neck. Eventually his fumbling fingers discover the top of a zip, and he gives it a great tug. But it seems to be caught. He turns his head

inside the mask and tries to squint down one nostril to see what's wrong. No good. He can't get round that far. He wrestles again with his gorilla head, sweating and miserable. It just won't come off.

There's nothing for it but to try and get some help. He remembers Ariadne. Wearily he makes his way right back along the alley-way to the Crazy Castle. He daren't walk along the prom for fear of meeting somebody. But when he gets there, to his surprise he finds the back door securely locked against him.

Charlie sits down on the doorstep, his mood of triumph turning to despair at the prospect of being imprisoned in this suit for much longer. He *must* find Ariadne. But then he remembers that Auntie Jean herself will still be at the launderette, which is quite near at hand in Market Street. She could hardly be all that cross with him for borrowing the gorilla costume, after his heroic adventures this evening. If only he can get there without meeting anyone. He searches behind Mr Cornetto's dustbin for his mackintosh and headscarf and puts them on, just in case. Then he sets off again.

He reaches the end of the alley-way and peers cautiously round the corner into Market Street. It's a quiet Sunday evening. Nobody is about. He hurries along the

street, keeping well in to the shop fronts and trying to hide his jutting gorilla jaw under the turned-up collar of his mackintosh. Suddenly Mrs Phillips from the bakery pops round the corner, with a carrier bag full of cakes for her sister up on the Penwyn Road. She runs straight into Charlie. They both stop short, face to face. Mrs Phillips lets out a piercing scream, like a factory siren, drops her bag, and scuttles away up the street, gobbling with fright. Doughnuts and iced fancies roll about all over the pavement. Ignoring them, Charlie hurries grimly on.

At last he sees the lights of the launderette, shining out into the street. He peers in through the window. Auntie Jean's still in there all right, idly turning the pages of a magazine while she waits for her wash. Nearby sit two ladies, deep in conversation, and a bored little boy who is gazing at the circular window of a washing-machine, with its whirling clothes, as raptly as if it were a television screen. Charlie edges towards the door, trying to capture Auntie Jean's attention, but it's the little boy who looks up first. They stare at one another silently.

"Mam," says the little boy presently.

"Yes, love."

"Look, Mam."

"Yes, what is it, then?"

"There's a gorilla."

"Oh, yes—lovely. Got your comic there, have you?"

"No, a gorilla, Mam. A real one. Out there in the street." He shakes her arm. "There, Mam."

Both ladies glance over to the door. But Charlie, of course, has shrunk back into the shadows.

"Ooh, a real gorilla. Just like the one on *Animal Magic*, isn't it?" says Mam fondly.

"No, this one's wearing a mac and a scarf thing over its head. But it's not there any more."

"Well, there's unusual. Mackintosh and scarf, is it? Well, I never did."

"I thought it was coming in here."

"I expect it's got some clothes for the wash, then," says Mam. Then lowering her voice to her friend: "He's that imaginative. Always full of fancies—the artistic type, you know."

Charlie, meanwhile, is becoming quite frantic. Auntie Jean won't look up. But the little boy is hanging over the back of his chair, waiting with interest for his reappearance. Now a young couple walk slowly towards him up the street, their arms draped about one another. Charlie, hunching deep into his collar, presses himself against the shop door. But they pass by, far too absorbed in each

other to notice him. At any moment somebody else will, though, thinks Charlie desperately.

At last Auntie Jean's drying-machine stops. She takes the clothes out, spending what seems like an endless and unnecessary time to fold each item carefully. Then she puts them back into the old pram and says good-night. The little boy watches her leave the shop with round eyes.

She is setting off briskly up the street when Charlie looms out of the darkness. She gasps and lets go of the pram handle, so that it nearly tips up over the curb.

"It's me, Auntie Jean," says Charlie plaintively. "I can't get out of this suit."

"Charlie! You did give me a turn! What, may I ask, are you doing out at this time of night dressed up like that? And where's Ariadne?"

"I don't know . . . I mean, I'll tell you all about it when we get home. But please help me out of this suit. I'm so sick of being inside it."

Clicking her tongue with exasperation, Auntie Jean fiddles with the back of Charlie's disguise.

"Drat the thing! It's no use. The zip's all caught up, and I haven't got my proper glasses. I'll have to take a pair of scissors to it when we get home."

"Come on then," says Charlie urgently, pulling her sleeve.

"But you can't walk home like that!" cries Auntie Jean. "What would we do if we met someone? What would the neighbours say? You're enough to give anyone heart failure with a face like that on you, indeed to goodness!"

Charlie decides to keep very quiet about Mrs Phillips from the bakery. Things are going to be difficult enough to explain as it is.

"I've got to get home somehow, Auntie Jean," he says.

Then Auntie Jean has one of her brainwaves.

"I know, you can get in the pram and hide under the washing. I can put the hood up so no one can see you."

"But . . ."

"Don't worry. The washing's bone dry."

"Oh all right . . ."

Charlie feels too tired to argue. Instead he climbs meekly into the big old pram and curls up with his knees jammed up against his chin, while Auntie Jean covers him with washing, careful to see that none of it gets dirty. It's surprisingly comfortable in there. So it isn't only

children who have the really daft ideas, thinks Charlie to himself, as Auntie Jean trundles him home.

Inside the launderette the little boy removes his nose from the glass door and climbs back on to his seat. He starts to shake his mother's arm again.

"Mam."

"Just a minute, dear. Don't interrupt when Mam's talking."

"But Mam . . ."

"What is it, then?"

"That gorilla."

"Oh, your gorilla. Not still here is it?"

"Oh no. It's gone. It went off in a pram with a lady pushing it."

"Oh yes, dear, so it did. Well never mind, it's past your bedtime."

As they pack up to go, Mam says to her friend:

"You know, sometimes I think they watch too much telly. But what can you do?"

10

During the next few days Mr Cornetto is busier than ever before. There are queues every night to get into the Crazy Castle, and even Auntie Jean's shop is doing a brisker trade. Besides local people and guests from the Hydro, parties start to come over from Penwyn, mostly made up of young people, all giggling with high spirits. Mysterious rumours are circulating that the old Crazy Castle really is haunted. It is whispered that strange things happen there after dark, that the waxwork figures hide more than meet the eye, and that lurking beast-like creatures pounce out at you if you're ever accidentally locked in there at night. Even Mr Cornetto himself is the focus of some curious stares and sidelong glances to see if, in spite of his jolly piano-playing and innocent moustache, he has Dracula fangs instead of teeth. The till, however, gets fuller and fuller as the money rattles in.

"Those Morgan boys won't come back, anyway," says Charlie for about the tenth time, as he and Ariadne hang over the rail at their favourite place at the end of the pier one morning. "I gave them a real scare. I told you I would, didn't I?"

Ariadne has been rather quiet since the evening of their adventure, and has found it difficult to go inside Mr Cornetto's Hall of Waxworks even in daylight, let alone in the dark.

"There *was* someone in there that night," she tells Charlie, also not for the first time. "Or else one of those waxworks moved by itself."

"Gerroff!" jeers Charlie, but he relents and adds, "Well, perhaps one did. But how could it? They're just plastic and wire and false hair when you get close up."

"How could *you* know what happened when you went off and left me all alone in there?" retorts Ariadne. "Typical of you, Charlie Moon," she can't resist adding.

"Well, I couldn't very well have stayed behind, could I? A fat lot of good that would have done."

Ariadne looks down at the waves, the colour of a fishmonger's green marble slab, patterned with white foam, endlessly heaving, lifting, and returning to slap the ironwork below their feet.

"Oh, well. You don't have to believe me if you don't want to," she says after a while. "I'm going back next week, anyway."

"So'm I."

"It'll be school again the week after."

"Yeah, worse luck. But better than being at home when Mum's in a bad mood, I suppose."

"I'm going to be a waitress at the Hydro on Saturday, though. Carnival Lunch—remember? I've got to wear this pathetic frilly apron. Why don't you come too, Charlie? The cook's all right. He's a friend of Mr Cornetto's. He'll let you stay in the kitchen. There'll be lots of food left over, I bet."

"Suppose the Old Moaner or the manageress finds me in there?"

"They'll be far too busy at the Lunch. There's going to be a Grand Surprise Bomb."

"An explosion, do you mean?" asks Charlie with interest.

"Not a real one. It's a kind of indoor firework made of coloured crinkle-paper. When you light it, it showers everyone with hundreds of thrilling surprises—paper hats, mottoes and novelties, or so it says on the label."

"Oh. I thought you meant real gunpowder."

"No, silly. It comes from Auntie Jean's shop, and it's going to be the centre-piece in the very middle of the room. It's been in her cupboard for heaven knows how long, and she's pleased as anything to have sold it at last.

There's going to be an orchestra, too."

"Sounds horrible," says Charlie.

"But you'll come?"

"Oh, all right, then, I'll come. Hey, it must be nearly lunch-time. We'd better be getting back to Auntie Jean's. I wish I had my skateboard here—it'd be great on this pier."

They walk back towards the prom, past the iron band-stand with the curly roof which is no longer used, and the rows of empty deck-chairs, flapping expectantly. Only a few holiday-makers are braving the wind, securely wrapped in anoraks and scarves, cheering themselves up with vacuum flasks of tea. Further up the pier are some shelters, glassed in on three sides, with seats back-to-back, separated by a high wooden partition. The side nearest to them is empty.

Charlie takes a run at it, and a flying leap on to the back of the seat, balancing along it as though it were a tight-rope. From this view-point his eyes are on a level with the top of the partition. He can just see over to the other side. There, below him, sits Miss Mona herself! She is so close that he could lean over and pat the top of her neatly waved head.

Charlie is so astonished that he stops still, swaying

slightly and gripping his perch with the soles of his baseball boots. Miss Mona isn't admiring the view. She has her back to him, hunched up and intent on something in her lap. She is putting something into what looks like a large envelope. Then she starts to lick it down. But suddenly as though she senses that she is being watched, she glances up. Her eyes meet Charlie's. In a moment, pushing whatever was in her hands into her handbag, she lunges round the shelter, thrusting her beak at Charlie like a vulture falling upon its prey.

"How *dare* you spy on me, you wretched boy? What do you mean by it? This is the third time I've caught you hanging about and making mischief. And what, may I ask, are *you* doing here?" she asks bitterly, catching sight of Ariadne.

Charlie jumps off the back of the seat and stands there awkwardly, too taken aback to answer. But Ariadne stands her ground.

"I'm sorry if we disturbed you, but we neither of us knew you were there as a matter of fact. We were just going back for lunch."

"Then what were you doing looking over that partition, then, tell me that?" demands Miss Mona, turning back to Charlie. Miserably, he takes off his cap, puts it on

back to front, removes it and puts it on again the right way round, well over the eyes. He is struck dumb.

But Ariadne answers for him in a clear voice:

"He never expected to see you there, and he certainly wasn't spying on you. So, if you'll excuse us, we must be getting back. We're not supposed to keep Auntie waiting for meals."

And, dragging Charlie by the arm, she marches off up the pier, leaving Miss Mona glaring angrily after them. They daren't look back until they have reached the prom. Miss Mona is still standing there, quite motionless, but by now they are too far away to see her expression. Once out of sight they both break into a run.

"Fancy you being able to get me out of that so easily," says Charlie, jogging along. "I'd never've had the nerve. That Old Moaner just scares me stiff."

"She doesn't scare me. It's only really scary things that scare me. She's just . . . well, typical. And I think she's the one that's acting a bit suspiciously if you ask me, not us."

"How do you mean? She only looked as if she was putting something into an envelope. Perhaps she was sending off seaside postcards to her friends, like we ought to be doing."

"Well, then, why should she get so cross about some-body seeing her?"

"Born cross, I suppose," says Charlie, "like so many of 'em are."

Auntie Jean and Mrs Cadwallader are reading the tea-leaves after lunch. Mrs Cadwallader's cup seems to be extra full of dramatic events.

"There's something really violent here," says Auntie Jean excitedly. "Looks like an explosion."

"Perhaps it's that Grand Surprise Bomb of yours," Ariadne suggests. She is lying on the sitting-room floor, using Einstein as a book-rest as usual. Charlie is drawing a monster with Ariadne's felt pens.

"Mona's temper, more like," says Mrs Cadwallader. "She's really on the warpath these days. She knows about our little sing-songs down at Carlo's place, of course. Everyone's talking about them up at the Hydro. It's driving her wild. She says I'm to stop it, and now she keeps going on at me about leaving here altogether. Just when I've started to enjoy myself for once."

"I can't see any sign of a journey here, Connie. But here's somebody running. It looks as though one person is chasing another."

"Really?" says Mrs Cadwallader with interest. "Go on, Jean."

"Some kind of a big upheaval in your life. I can't quite make it out. And here's some rings and a necklace, too, very plain."

"That'll be my pearls."

"Well, I hope you've put them away safely, now, Connie," says Auntie Jean sternly, putting down the teacup. "Let these tea-leaves be a warning to you. Fancy leaving them in the Hall of Waxworks like that! And with all these burglars about. It was a wonder you didn't lose them for good, indeed."

"I do try, Jean," says Mrs Cadwallader, carelessly lighting a cigarette. "I know I'm hopelessly absent-minded. But it was Caddy's family jewellery, you know—it's not as though he'd bought it for me himself. I'd take more care of it if he had, more sentimental value. But it just doesn't seem to mean much to me, somehow. The pearls belonged to his mother, of course. Those two rings that Charlie found were hers, too."

"Three," says Charlie, without looking up from his drawing.

"What, dear?"

"There were three rings. I remember."

"Well, I only seem to have got the two now. I suppose I must have left the other one somewhere since. Oh dear, don't tell Mona whatever you do! She'll be *furious* with me. I'll never hear the end of it. She's being difficult enough as it is. That reminds me—what's the time? I must fly. She's expecting me."

"I'll be at the Carnival Lunch tomorrow," Auntie Jean tells her, as she gathers up the cups and plates. "Special invitation from the manageress, see, as I've supplied the Grand Surprise Bomb, and the crackers too. They're my best stock—very expensive ones. I thought I was never going to get rid of them."

"That crowd at the Hydro are going to need more than crackers to get them going if you ask me," says Mrs Cadwallader putting on her coat. "Well, I'm off. Cheerio. See you at the party. And if Mona's in her present mood, Heaven help us all!"

11

Charlie is hiding in the Hydro Hotel kitchen. The cook and the chief waitress, Winnie Probert, are prepared to put up with him only if he keeps well out of their way. So he has found a good place for himself between the cupboard where the knives and forks are kept, and the service doors which lead into the dining-room. These have little port-hole shaped windows in them, and flap open and shut continuously as Winnie and Ariadne, frilly-aproned and already red in the face with exertion, rush to and fro. On the kitchen side of the doors all is in turmoil, with Winnie and the cook screaming orders at one another in Welsh and darting about, dealing out plates as rapidly as if they were playing-cards. On the dining-room side of the door, Winnie instantly slows down to a dignified pace, gliding among the tables as though she were on castors, and giving her instructions quietly to Ariadne in English, as they gracefully distribute the half-grapefruits, each with its glacé cherry, to every place.

Now and then, when the manageress isn't about, Charlie can get a peep through the port-hole in the door, to watch the guests assembling. They sit at small tables,

each with a white cloth, a silver vase of carnations, and a cracker by each plate. Most of the Hydro residents are rather sedate, and there are not nearly enough of them to fill the huge dining-room. Conversation is hushed, and in the long pauses in between they look about as though challenging the management to create in them a mood of Carnival gaiety.

In the centre of the room, with a table all to itself, is Auntie Jean's Grand Surprise Bomb, done out in frills of bright pink, yellow and green paper. Auntie Jean herself is in red, her favourite colour. Mrs Cadwallader wears dazzling orange and a great deal of jewellery. They sit at a table with Miss Mona, Colonel Quickly, and little Miss Mellish. The Colonel resembles a trim grey bull-terrier, and he is not in the habit of wasting words. His clipped moustache bristles aggressively as he attacks his half-grapefruit. Although little Miss Mellish does her best to chirp and squeak enthusiastically, conversation is difficult. Everyone is relieved when a musical quartet, consisting of three thin ladies, playing stringed instruments, and one very large one at the piano, strikes up on a platform at one end of the room.

The manageress appears and moves smilingly from one table to another, as though to rally the guests into

enjoying themselves. Ariadne, concentrating hard so as not to drop anything, comes round with the next course—bits of chicken, rigidly set in a kind of yellow jelly, salad and potatoes. Mrs Cadwallader is plainly bored. She picks at her food, and complains that she doesn't like the tunes that the quartet are playing, and says that they haven't any go.

"Ah, you professionals!" cries little Miss Mellish, wagging her finger playfully. "We mustn't forget you're an entertainer yourself, Mrs Cadwallader. I hear you've been having a great success down on the prom . . ."

But, catching Miss Mona's eye, she realizes that she has somehow said the wrong thing, and immediately changes the subject. By the time the trifle comes round, things have not improved. The quartet are fiddling away at a breakneck pace, valiantly trying to fill the huge echoing room with festive sound. Ariadne has been running with trays for nearly an hour, but she has managed to smuggle four helpings of trifle to Charlie in his vantage-point behind the door.

The party at Mrs Cadwallader's table have finished eating at last. Mrs Cadwallader lights up a cigarette in her long green holder, and puffs away moodily.

"I hope you'll forgive me for saying so, but I do so

admire that ring," pipes little Miss Mellish, still struggling to keep the conversation going. "The one with the green stone. It's a very unusual setting, I think."

"My ring?" says Mrs Cadwallader, idly holding out her hand, which flashes with jewels. "Oh, this one, d'you mean?"

"Yes. How very pretty it is."

"That one's been in my poor dear husband's family for many years," says Mrs Cadwallader, taking off the ring and holding it up to the light so that Miss Mellish can see it better. "It's the most valuable of the lot, as a matter of fact."

"Oh, how interesting!" says Miss Mellish, peering short-sightedly.

At this moment their conversation is cut short. The quartet have come to the end of a piece, and play a great flourishing chord. The manageress holds up her hands for silence in the centre of the room.

"Now, ladies and gentlemen, it's the moment you've all been waiting for! If you're all ready, I am going to light the Grand Surprise Bomb so stand by for thrills!"

And with a dramatic gesture she lights the fuse on the big paper confection. There is a hush. The guests, turning from their coffee cups, watch expectantly as the

Grand Surprise Bomb splutters and hisses into life. A bitter smell fills the air. This is followed by some spurts of light, rather like a firework which can't make up its mind whether to stop or start. The coloured paper is slowly turning brown and curling at the edges. Now—*pop, pop, pop!* Some streamers and small objects, wrapped in coloured paper, shoot upwards and roll away over the dining-room floor. Some of the more sporting guests bend down to pick them up, discovering inside some paper hats, whistles and one or two small plastic toys. Miss Mellish unwraps a paper bonnet, which she laughingly puts on, tying the ribbons under her chin.

But Auntie Jean is beginning to look anxious. The smell is getting worse. One or two of the guests are forced to hold handkerchiefs to their noses. Some more coloured lights fly up, and one or two more parcels, but these are steadily followed by a lot of brown smoke, which drifts and billows across the room. The fleeting mood of festivity quickly gives way to one of dismay. People are coughing, their eyes streaming. The manageress flaps at the smoke with a table-napkin, but this only seems to make matters worse. She signals frantically to the quartet, who start to play again, a rousing overture this time. But the guests are retreating

to the other end of the room to avoid the smoke, which by this time is so dense they can hardly see one another.

"Quick, get the handyman!" the manageress tells Winnie desperately. "We'll have to put it out, or we'll all be suffocated!"

"The Grand Surprise Bomb's going up in smoke," Ariadne tells Charlie, dashing through the service doors. "Isn't that just too absolutely *pathetic*! And that isn't all. I've just seen . . ."

But Charlie, who has been watching events with interest through the port-hole in the door, has had one of his good ideas. He picks up a huge jug of lemonade, which he has noticed on the table, and puts it into Ariadne's hands.

"Here, pour that over it," he tells her.

Ariadne, who has great faith in Charlie in these sort of circumstances, doesn't hesitate for a moment. She runs back into the dining-room and promptly empties the entire contents of the jug over the Grand Surprise Bomb. There is a sizzling noise, and an even worse smell than before, but gradually the flow of brown smoke decreases, and then dies away altogether, leaving lemonade seeping all over the table and dripping into a puddle on the floor below. The remains of the bomb are

now just a mass of charred and sodden crinkle-paper.

It takes time and a great deal of reassurance from the manageress to persuade the guests to reassemble. Two ladies have been overcome by nervous hysteria and have had to be helped to their rooms. The handyman appears with a bucket and mop, and he and Winnie start to clear up the mess. Meanwhile the quartet plays on, one jolly tune after another without a break. But by now the Carnival Lunch is a definite failure. Auntie Jean is trying hard not to catch the manageress's eye. The crackers lie abandoned on the tables with the cold cups of coffee. Nobody has the heart to pull them.

"Now, if you would all like to . . ." begins the manageress, in her brightest voice, but she is interrupted by a loud cry from Mrs Cadwallader:

"Where's my ring?" she says.

12

The eyes of everyone in the room are turned to Mrs Cadwallader.

"I know I had it just before that horrible bomb thing went off and gave us all such a fright," she tells them. "I think I must have dropped it somewhere . . ."

"Oh dear, oh dear, I'm sure it's my fault!" cries Miss Mellish, her paper bonnet quivering apologetically. "You wouldn't have taken it off if I hadn't admired it just now. Then this would never have happened."

At this moment, Colonel Quickly, who until now has not given any sign of enjoying himself, takes the matter in hand. Briskly he declares that the ring *must* be found. With a few brief orders he organizes the guests into a search-party, and a great hunt begins. Every inch of the floor round the table is searched, plates carefully inspected, and coffee cups checked. This proves fruitless.

"Turn out your handbag, Connie," suggests Auntie Jean. "You might have put it in there. You know how absent-minded you are."

Mrs Cadwallader tips out her large handbag on to the table, but no ring appears.

"I think," says Colonel Quickly in a quiet but deter-

mined voice, "that we should all of us, who were sitting round this table, agree to turn out our pockets and handbags for the manageress to inspect."

There is an awkward pause.

"Surely, Colonel, you're not suggesting . . ." says the manageress. "I mean, there's no question of theft, of course."

"A formality only," says the Colonel, holding up his hand. "It's as well to have these matters cleared up right away."

"Oh, yes! I'd *so* much rather we did," agrees Miss Mellish. "I was sitting next to Mrs Cadwallader, and I feel so *responsible*, really."

"Very well, as a formality," says the manageress.

The Colonel is the first to turn out his pockets, methodically placing each item side by side on the table—his wallet, loose change, watch and chain, and a beautifully laundered clean handkerchief. Then it's Auntie Jean's turn. She has no pockets, but her handbag is full of an astonishing number of things—playing-cards, used bus tickets, old photographs, hairpins, bits of a broken electric plug, all come tumbling out. And now Miss Mellish carefully lays out the contents of her embroidery bag, full of a profusion of coloured silks, and

her tiny purse, only big enough to contain one or two personal items.

"Come on, Mona, your turn now," says Mrs Cadwallader cheerfully. She seems to be the only person in the dining-room to be relatively unconcerned about the loss of the ring, and she, too, has started to enjoy herself. Miss Mona says nothing. She is rather pale. Haughtily she puts down her handbag on the table, opens the clasp, and stands back while the manageress searches through the contents.

"There's nothing here, of course," says the manageress as she hands it back to her. "Thank you all the same, Miss Mona. And now, ladies and gentlemen, I really don't think there's any need to keep you all here any longer. I'm sorry our Carnival Lunch has ended with this little . . . er . . . difficulty. But I have asked the quartet to play to you instead in the Palm Lounge this afternoon—so if you would all care to clear the dining-room . . ."

"Hey, Charlie, you'd better get out of here quickly," says Ariadne urgently, reappearing through the service doors. "The manageress is coming this way. She'll be wanting us to turn out our pockets next, I expect. But don't go away. I *must* talk to you."

"Where'll I hide?" says Charlie.

"There's a little room full of buckets and brooms and things just near the tradesmen's entrance," Ariadne tells him. "She'll never find you in there. There's something I've just got to do, but I'll come as soon as I can."

The guests of the Hydro have mostly drifted into the Palm Lounge, to listen to the music, and complain to one another in undertones about the events of the day so far. Mrs Cadwallader, Miss Mona and Auntie Jean are sitting in basket chairs in a corner of the deserted veranda which overlooks the sea. The two friends are still discussing the possible whereabouts of Mrs Cadwallader's ring, but Miss Mona is very silent.

"I hope it's insured," says Auntie Jean. "The way you keep getting it mislaid, it certainly ought to be."

"Er . . . well . . . as a matter of fact, I'm not sure that it is. I know I should have remembered to keep up the payments, but somehow it kept slipping my mind."

"But supposing it has been stolen? Surely it's a matter for the police?"

"The police? Well, I suppose it'll have to be, if it doesn't turn up."

But Miss Mona suddenly starts to her feet, white-faced with agitation.

"Oh, no, Connie! Not the police!" she says. "I mean . . . think of all the trouble . . . the questions, publicity, even . . ."

"But, Mona, how else are we going to find out where it is?"

"I'll tell you, if you like," says a voice behind them.

They all look up in surprise. There stands Ariadne, still wearing her apron, with Charlie looking over her shoulder.

"And where have you two come from, indeed?" asks Auntie Jean. "And what do you mean, exactly, Ariadne, if we may ask?"

"I know where your ring is, Mrs Cadwallader," answers Ariadne. "It's inside a cracker."

"A *cracker*? What on earth is the child on about!" cries Mrs Cadwallader.

"Yes, one of the crackers that was on your table at lunch-time. And, what's more, I'm afraid I know who put it there."

At this moment a truly terrible thing happens. Miss Mona comes forward with clenched fists, and Ariadne, as though expecting an attack, shrinks back towards

Charlie for support. But there is no attack. Miss Mona simply covers her face with her hands and starts to sob. For a moment they all look at her, quite at a loss to know what to do. But Mrs Cadwallader is soon at her side, with an arm round her heaving shoulders.

"There now, Mona. Come along, now, this isn't like you. Just you sit down, now, and tell us all about it."

Miss Mona collapses into a basket chair and cries bitterly for a long time. In stricken silence, they all wait for her to recover herself enough to speak. At last, painfully, her words come:

"Oh, Connie, the child is telling the truth. I can't deny it. I took your ring when you left it lying on the table, and hid it in my handbag."

"*You* took my ring, Mona?" echoes Mrs Cadwallader, hardly able to believe her ears.

"Yes. Then, when the Colonel suggested that we all submit to a search, I . . . I was terrified. I thought I was going to be exposed as a thief, in front of everyone. So I slipped it into the cracker beside my plate. It was the only way I could think of to avoid being found out. I just couldn't have borne it—but now . . ."

"But Mona . . ." Mrs Cadwallader interrupts her, "I don't understand. Why on earth . . .?"

Miss Mona puts a shaking hand on to her arm. "I'll try to explain. It's so difficult, but I'll try. I owe you all an explanation. I took the ring, and other bits of jewellery too, when you left them lying about. But I'm not a thief! I never intended to take them for myself, Connie. In fact, they're all safely in your bank."

"In the bank? You mean, *you* sent them there?"

"Yes. To stop them really being stolen, by someone else, or from being lost for ever. You were so careless, Connie. All these years you've been wearing the jewellery that Caddy left you—the jewellery that was my mother's, that has been in our family for generations—and I've had to sit by and watch you leave it about, and lose it as though it was so much rubbish . . ."

And Miss Mona starts to cry afresh. Auntie Jean and the children look at the ground, embarrassed by her distress, not knowing what to say. Mrs Cadwallader silently pats her hand for a while.

"Mona," she says at last, "I've been a real pig—a selfish pig! Fancy me not noticing how much you minded about it, all this time. You're right about my being careless, too. Why, I'd have *given* you the whole lot, if you'd only asked me!"

"It wasn't for me to ask, Connie. You were Caddy's

wife, after all. I just took a brooch or a necklace here and there whenever you left it lying about. And when this boy here returned three of your rings, I kept just one, so that I could send it to the bank for safe-keeping, and gave you back the other two—and you never noticed! Then you mentioned—so unconcerned you were about it, Connie—that you'd left your pearls in that awful waxwork place. Heaven knows what might have happened to them there . . ."

"I found them," puts in Auntie Jean. "And I returned them to Connie, of course."

"I didn't know. I thought if I could get hold of them without you noticing, Connie, I could rescue them, too. I *knew* you'd lose them in the end. So I . . . I went down there the other evening when you were all out. I found the back door open . . ."

"That was the night we chased the Morgan boys—" gasps Charlie.

"—and I saw one of the waxworks move," says Ariadne. "It must've been you!"

"Yes, I know I frightened you. I kept very still among the waxworks at first, hoping that you wouldn't discover me there when you came in. I was so confused. I didn't know what to do, you see. But in the end, I thought I'd

better show myself. I was trying to pluck up courage to tell you I was there, but you ran away before I could speak!"

"There! I *told* you, didn't I?" says Ariadne, rounding on Charlie. "And you wouldn't believe me. *Typical!*"

"But now we must get your ring back out of that cracker, Connie, or I'll never forgive myself, never!" says Miss Mona.

"Well, that's going to be jolly difficult," says Ariadne. They all turn to her.

"Why?" asks Miss Mona in a faint voice.

"I knew about it being in the cracker—I saw you put it there when I was being a waitress, you see—and I went back as soon as I could, after everyone had gone, to rescue it, so's I could give it back to Mrs Cadwallader. But it was no good. Because, you see, the manageress had already told Winnie to put all the crackers back into the boxes. And, as they're all the same on the outside, by the time I got there you couldn't tell which was which. So that's why I came to fetch you. You'd better all come as quickly as you can!"

13

They all run to the dining-room. It is empty of guests. The tables are cleared, and no trace of the Carnival remains. They find Winnie in the kitchen, her feet up on a chair, drinking a cup of tea.

"Oh, yes. The manageress told me to put the crackers back in the boxes and take them to her office. Took a lot of extra time, too, as though we haven't had enough for one day, indeed, and me run off my feet as it is."

They hurry back into the hall and knock urgently on the glass door of the office. The manageress appears, rather short-tempered, as though she, too, has had enough for one day.

"The crackers? You're too late, I'm afraid. I couldn't see any further use for them, unless we put them away till Christmas, but that's a long time. So I sent the handyman down with them to St Ethelred's—the children's holiday home, you know. I told him to give them to the children with the compliments of the Hydro."

Miss Mona lets out a wild cry.

"Children? You mean you've given them all away?"

"Yes, I've just told you. They're going back to-

morrow, I believe, and they're having a little party, so I thought I'd . . ."

But her words are lost as they stampede past her towards the front door.

"It's down this way, where the beach-huts are at the end of the prom," says Auntie Jean, breathlessly taking the lead. They all follow her, dodging the holiday-makers through the narrow streets to where St Ethelred's stands, down by the shore. A large expanse of coarse sea-grass and sand slopes down before it and merges with the beach itself. There are no children playing on the dangling rope-ladders, motor-tyres, and complicated structures of planks and brightly painted steel. But their voices, and the sound of very loud music, can be heard through the open windows. They race up the front steps, and ring the doorbell. Nobody answers. The doors stand open. Auntie Jean leads the way into a large bare hall, and, for a moment, they all stand there, panting, at a loss to know what to do next.

At last a student helper appears carrying a large tray full of plastic beakers and sodden drinking straws.

"Crackers?" he says doubtfully, as Auntie Jean tries, not very successfully, to explain the situation in a few clear words. "Oh, yes. But I'm afraid it's going to be

difficult to help you. We've had the crackers. The kids pulled them all after tea. Some of them are still in there . . ." He jerks his head in the direction of the noise . . . "the others have gone down on to the beach."

They enter the big room, where a great many children are bobbing, bouncing, and skidding about on the linoleum, to the accompaniment of a record-player, which is turned up to full blast. Everywhere beneath their feet, amongst the bits of squashed sandwich, sweet-papers, and other party wreckage, lie remnants of the crackers. One or two of them, left unpulled, have been torn open down the middle so that the contents could be removed. All the children have paper hats, and they are all wearing sparkling fake jewellery.

"There was a ring in nearly every cracker," says Auntie Jean faintly. "Rings, necklaces, or brooches, and watches too. Riddles and mottoes. They were my deluxe ones, you see."

Miss Mona covers her face with her hands again.

"Well, we'd better start searching," says Mrs Cadwallader grimly.

Dai and Dylan Morgan are sitting behind the beach-huts—a favourite place of theirs, well away from prying

eyes. Dai's cheeks are bulging with sweets, which he is popping into his mouth, two at a time, from a paper bag. Dylan is idling with the contents of a large pocket handkerchief which is spread across his knees.

"We've got lots of stuff here—brooches, watches, necklaces, rings, and lots of riddles," he says, rattling them all about together.

"Well, never mind the riddles—they're daft," Dai tells him, dribbling stickily out of the corner of his mouth. "You can throw them out for a start."

Dylan does so, crumpling them all up into a tight ball and throwing it on to the sand. The wind catches it, and scatters the bits of paper among the sea-grass which grows between the backs of the beach-huts and the sea-wall. They have had a very successful afternoon, so far, lying in wait for the smaller children from St Ethelred's and bullying them into parting with their sweets and cracker surprises. Dai is particularly fond of sweet things, but he doesn't care to buy his own as it's so much more fun getting them off someone else for nothing. The cracker things are not so interesting. They have thrown them all carelessly into Dylan's handkerchief, to be examined later, at leisure.

"Hey, I've nearly finished this lot," says Dai, looking into the bottom of his bag. "Time we tried to get some more. Should be easy. Like they say 'easier than taking sweets off a kid'. Heh! Heh!"

Dylan knots up his handkerchief and puts it down on the sand. He eases himself slyly through the gap between the beach-huts. Sure enough, the children from St Ethelred's are still there, some of them playing quite close at hand.

"Here, you!" calls Dai, whistling softly.

One of the little boys, alone with a sandcastle, stops digging and looks up.

"Yeah, you. Got something for you."

The little boy puts down his spade, and, holding on to his paper hat to stop it from blowing away, trots obediently across the beach towards them. Once he is within range, Dylan shoots out a hand, grabs the front of his T-shirt, and drags him behind the hut.

"Got some sweets there, have you?" says Dai, now also on his feet. He throws away his empty bag. Then he tweaks the little boy's paper hat off his head and throws that away, too.

"I've eaten mine," says the little boy, hiding his hands behind his back. "What've you got to show me, then?"

"Show you nothing," grins Dai. "*You* show *us*—what you've got there."

"It's mine. They gave it me. They said we could keep our things out of the crackers and take them home."

"Show us, I said."

"Don't want to."

Then Dai puts his face very close to the little boy's, and says in a quiet voice:

"If you don't show us, d'you know what we're going to do?"

The little boy doesn't answer. He purses up his mouth bravely, to stop his lower lip from wobbling.

"Well, I'll tell you," murmurs Dai. "We've got the key to this beach-hut, see. And we're going to put you in there and lock the door and go away, so you'll be in there all night, see. There's no light in there. And what's more, if we don't decide to come and let you out tomorrow morning, you might miss the train home. And then what will your Mam do?"

The little boy starts to screw up his eyes, which are filling with tears. He brings out his hands from behind his back and offers up, on his wrist, a pretend watch, studded with jewels, with a pink plastic face.

"Let's have it then . . ." says Dai.

But before he can wrench it off, there's a slithering noise, a soft thud, and Charlie Moon drops down from the sea-wall, landing lightly, just beside them. The Morgan boys look round for an instant in surprise, and the little boy takes his opportunity at once. As quick as a flash, he darts round the hut and is away up the beach, running towards the safety of the others, his twinkling legs kicking up the sand in all directions but his watch still firmly on his wrist.

Balked of their prey, the Morgan boys turn menacingly on Charlie.

"What's this, then?" says Dai. "Spying on us, were you, boy? Creeping on the sea-wall up there without us knowing?"

"Yes, I was," says Charlie carelessly. "Looking for you, really."

Dylan's hand has already closed on his shoulder.

"Looking for us, is it? Want to tell us what for, boy?"

"I've got some things to sell. They were given to me, and I don't really want them, but I don't like to say so, you see. Wondered if you'd like to do a deal."

At this last word, Dylan's hand relaxes slightly.

"What've you got, then?" he asks promptly. "Got it here?"

"It's just up at my Auntie's. It's an underwater mask and snorkel, almost new. They're really good—came from a big London shop. My Mum paid pounds for them."

"What d'you want for them?"

"Well, how much'll you give me?"

"Not worth much to us. Don't do much swimming, do we, Dai?"

"You could sell them, though," says Charlie casually. There is a small pause.

"Trouble is, we haven't got much cash," says Dai.

"Not more'n a few pence," says Dylan.

"Spent it all," says Dai.

"Pity. I've got a whole box of stink-bombs, and some itching powder—the sort that really works," says Charlie. "I might throw them in, too."

Dylan can't resist showing a little interest. He picks up his handkerchief and starts to undo the knot.

"We've got some valuable stuff here, though," he says winking at his brother. "Real jewellery, it is. We found it, like. Came by it accidentally, didn't we, Dai?"

"It doesn't look real to me," says Charlie, barely glancing into the handkerchief, which they are holding out for him to see.

"It's the truth. Good stuff, it is—worth a lot."

"Well . . ."

"I'll throw in this 50p then," says Dai, feeling in his back pocket. "Didn't know I had it on me . . ."

"Oh, all right," says Charlie, "I might as well, I suppose. You'll have to come up to my Auntie's and wait outside while I get the things."

Dai and Dylan manage to contain themselves until Charlie has duly fetched all the things he has promised, and they are well out of sight up the prom with them, before doubling up with laughter.

"He swallowed it!" crows Dai. "Fell right into it, didn't he!"

"The way we conned him!" chuckles Dylan. "Easier than doing those little kids back there. It's a good mask and snorkel set, too. We can sell it for a good few quid to Gomer Roberts, the sports shop. And we can have some fun with the other stuff ourselves."

"He must be even dafter than he looks," gasps Dai, tears of mirth rolling down his cheeks. "Fancy him thinking all that rubbish was *real jewellery*!"

Back at Auntie Jean's, Charlie is already carefully emptying out the contents of Dylan's handkerchief on to

the table. Amongst all the glittering hoard, one piece is heavier than the others. The green stone takes the light as he holds it up.

Mrs Cadwallader's ring is safe at last.

14

It's Charlie and Ariadne's last evening at Auntie Jean's. They are leaving on the first train in the morning, and their suitcases are already packed. Mrs Cadwallader, Mr Cornetto and even Miss Mona have arrived for a special celebration supper, to say good-bye. Mrs Cadwallader is quite tearfully sentimental about everything, especially about Charlie, so much so that he is inwardly anxious in case she decides to sing a song to mark the occasion. Even if she does, however, he's in no position to complain. The cash reward she has given to him, and to Ariadne, for their part in saving her ring, has been very generous. On top of this, she has promised to replace his underwater mask and snorkel with the very best ones that money can buy, or anything else in the shop that might take his fancy.

"He's a brave lad—a clever, brave lad," she keeps saying, putting her arm round his shoulders. "Make a good detective when you grow up, you would, an' all!"

"It wasn't all that difficult," says Charlie modestly. "I just spotted the Morgan boys from the top of the sea-wall while you were all still searching for the ring up at the house. Some of the little kids had told me they were

around somewhere, taking their sweets and cracker presents. I wasn't sure that they'd got your ring, of course. But I just knew I had to get the stuff back from them so I could find out. I couldn't fight them because they're both so much bigger than me. So I took a chance on doing a swop. It was pretending not to be too eager that was the hardest part."

"Wouldn't they be *sick* if they knew they'd got hold of a real emerald amongst all that cracker jewellery and never realized it," says Ariadne.

"Well, I suppose they never will, now, so good riddance to them," says Auntie Jean. "But I hope you're not going to leave that ring lying about anywhere else, after all this, Connie."

Mrs Cadwallader only laughs.

"That's not my worry any more, Jean," she says. "As a matter of fact, I've given all the family jewellery back to Mona. She's much better at looking after it, aren't you, Mona?"

"It's very good of you, Connie," says Miss Mona. "I won't be wearing it in the ordinary way, of course. I intend to keep it carefully in the bank, where I know it's safe. But I do have to thank this resourceful boy here. I'm very sorry about the . . . er . . . unpleasantness

we've had in the past, and I do hope that you'll forgive and forget."

"Won't you miss wearing all that jewellery, Connie?" asks Auntie Jean rather wistfully.

Mrs Cadwallader beams girlishly across at Mr Cornetto.

"Oh, no. I'll still have one ring of my own that I'll be taking the *greatest* care of, won't I, Carlo? You see, I'm settling down in Penwyn Bay for good."

Here Mr Cornetto, who has been very quiet until now, gets to his feet, smooths back his hair, adjusts his butterfly tie, and stands up to attention like a general on parade.

"I think it's now time that I told you all our good news. Mrs Cadwallader . . . Connie . . . has done me the great honour of consenting to be my wife!"

The cries of surprise and joy, hugs, embraces and pumping handshakes that follow this announcement go on for a long time. Even Miss Mona, in her newly relaxed mood, seems pleased. She has been thinking for a long time, she says, of settling down herself in some really *refined* place—in a little flat of her own, perhaps. The conversation falls into an excited discussion of plans—wedding plans, house redecoration plans, plans

for the Crazy Castle, hats and dresses, of course . . .

After a while, Charlie and Ariadne slip away unnoticed. It's nearly dark when they reach their favourite place at the end of the pier. They hang over the rail, looking far out to sea. A little wind is blowing up, and a long ribbon of pale lemon sky marks the place where the sea ends and the huge night sky begins. One or two stars are out already.

"Fancy them getting *married*," says Ariadne. "I never thought they'd do a thing like that. Absolutely pathetic! Still, she was pretty good about our rewards."

"What are you going to do with yours?" asks Charlie.

"I'm putting it into my Escape Fund, of course."

"Escape from what?"

"Well, everything. Being a grown-up and doing boring things and going on about the good old days. I won't need it till I've left school, of course. I've got my wages as well, from being a waitress at the Hydro—the manageress gave me an extra tip for putting out the Grand Surprise Bomb—so it's getting on quite nicely. What about you?"

"I'm thinking about being a detective when I grow up, like she said," answers Charlie, "not a famous actor, as I've been planning. Perhaps I'll ask her to get me a

detective set instead of a new underwater mask and
snorkel. I saw a smashing one in the shop where I went
with Mum. It had handcuffs, and a magnifying-glass, and
stuff for taking fingerprints, and everything. I think I'll
go and have another look at it first thing on Mon-
day . . ."

The ribbon of lemon sky is gradually getting narrower.
At last it disappears altogether.

"Of course, I might find that I need the Escape Fund
before I'm grown up," says Ariadne dreamily.

"It's got false eyebrows and moustaches and all,"
Charlie goes on. "And wigs, all different colours . . ."

"I dare say they'll come in handy whatever you decide
to be," says Ariadne.